xo,

Melissa

Goodbye Hales

Acknowledgements

Thank YOU! Thank you for reading my book and for taking a chance on a new author!

Thank you to my friends and family for all of their support, especially my husband and son. Y'all are the best!

Thank you to my pre-readers. I couldn't do it without you guys giving me feedback and telling me to hurry up and write more! (Kate Vandagriff, Brooke Trimble, Leitasha Scott, Paige Yearby, Anisha Pineda, Kaysie Bishop)

Thank you, Ann, with AJ Field Editing for polishing this story.

Thank you to Mikayla Nichols and Alec Iacovelli (Instagram: @yaboii_ai) for being my cover models. Both of you are perfect!

Last, but definitely not least, THANK YOU, Kaysie Bishop. Thank you for being the best photographer I know. Thank you for figuring out how to make the perfect book cover. And thank you for making this so much fun.

Payton

I looked past the entrance but couldn't get my feet to budge. The man, I assumed, drove the car that brought me here, took my backpack, and carried it inside.

"C'mon in, Payton. Take a look around."

"Where am I?" I whispered. Apparently I had been asleep since we pulled out of the airport in Dallas.

"You're in Alabama, sweetheart. Your new home sweet home."

I closed my eyes and tried to swallow the lump in my throat before walking inside. I stood close to the doorway, fighting the urge to run back to the car and haul ass back to California.

"I put your suitcases in the bedroom on the left. It's the biggest of the two," the man said.

I nodded so he knew I was listening. But I couldn't make myself speak. What would *Payton* say?

"Ya know, my granddaughter is about your age. I could have her take ya into town and show ya around a bit, if ya like?"

"I think I'm going to keep to myself for a few days. You know, to adjust and what not," I answered as politely as I could.

"Understood ma'am. I guess I best be going. I put my card on your suitcase. Call if ya need anything."

"Thank you," I mumbled as he walked out the door.

"Oh, I almost forgot. Your friend brought your car by yesterday. It's in the garage."

I don't know if I was more stunned at the knowledge of having a car or a friend. After watching me stand there open-mouthed, the man tipped his hat and drove away in his patrol car.

Once he had disappeared down the gravel road, I rushed inside and locked the door. I was finally alone. It had been a long fourteen days since I'd had any time by myself. I felt relieved, but I was scared.

After several calming breaths, I made my way to the garage. A fairly used Jeep Wrangler was parked inside. I opened the driver's side door and saw the keys lying in the front seat next to the hand-held garage door opener. The Jeep wasn't anything special compared to the Cadillac CTS I'd had back home, but at least they got me something black.

I slid behind the wheel and adjusted my seat and mirrors, intending on taking it for a test drive. When I turned my head to look out the back window as the garage door was rising, however, I froze.

A brand new infant car seat was buckled into the middle of my backseat. My hand instinctively went down to rest on my three months along baby bump.

The baby carrier was light grey and yellow, which was perfect seeing as how I didn't know the sex of my baby yet. I had a feeling it was going to be a boy, but that was no guarantee. A few tears fell onto my cheeks as I pictured a little boy with his dad's light hair and my dark eyes.

When I was told I was going to be relocated for my safety, I had already lost everyone in my life. Especially when they told me I would have to change my identity.

I would never see any of the agents who had worked my case again, and that meant I would never know who to thank for the car or the baby seat. So I said my thanks out loud in the new-to-me Jeep for nobody to hear. Still, I felt better.

After unpacking the few clothes I was able to bring along, I showered and got as comfortable as possible on the couch. I had a bed in one of the bedrooms, the bigger one that the police officer had put my suitcases in. It had plain white sheets with a light purple comforter, and the room was completely bare other than the small dresser I had put my clothes in. At least on the couch I had the TV to keep me company.

I made a mental to-do list before I dozed off listening to the local news.

1. Find a job
2. Buy food for the house
3. Buy new bed sheets and comforter

***

"What do you want?" I snapped.

"Haley, I know you hate me right now, but please do not hang up the phone," Sean frantically begged.

"Sean, what is going on?" I asked, annoyed that he was calling me so late. Or calling me at all, for that matter.

"I fucked up, Hales. I fucked up, and now they're coming for you and your family. They've already got Josh. I'm so fucking sorry, Haley."

"What? Who's coming? Who's got Josh?"

"Hide, Hales. You've got to hide! Now! Protect yourself!"

I could hear him crying on the other end of the phone, but I didn't move a muscle. I couldn't. Shock had taken over my body.

"Sean, what did you do? What did you do?!" I screamed.

Before he could answer, I heard the cracking of the front door being kicked in downstairs. Adrenaline kicked in after that. I jumped out of bed in nothing but a tank top and my underwear. The hand that wasn't holding my phone to my ear clung to my baby bump in effort to protect the life inside of me.

I slowly walked to my bedroom door. With a shaky hand, I twisted the knob. I could hear my mother crying down the hall. That meant they had already made it upstairs. Without thinking for a second longer, I ran down the hall and locked myself in the bathroom.

I could hear Sean yelling through the phone as I sat against the bathroom door crying. Waiting for them to take me, too.

"Haley! Where are you?! Haley!"

"I'm in the bathroom, Sean. There's nowhere for me to go. They'll find me soon," I mumbled between sobs.

"The cops are coming. You have to get out of the house. You still have time. You can do this, Haley."

I had my mother's hair dryer in my hand before he was finished talking. The first time I hit the window, nothing happened. I knew that everyone in the house heard it, though. So I swung again, harder. The half-sized window was only meant to let natural light in. I've never been more thankful for my tiny body than in that moment.

My bare feet hit the shingles below me with a thud. I saw the lights of several police cars coming over the hill. They would be here soon.

I tiptoed to the opposite side of the house. There was a tree that had been hanging over my parents' roof for as long as I can remember. I had climbed that tree a thousand times growing up, but it had recently been trimmed so that no branches were within reaching distance. I knew I was going to have to jump.

"Sean, I'm safe. I'm going to make it, but I have to hang up."

"I'll be dead by morning, Hales. I'm so fucking sorry. I know I caused all of this. I'm sorry I couldn't be the man you needed me to be, and I'm sorry I couldn't love the baby like you do. You're going to be a good mom. Stay safe. I love you."

I choked on a sob and he hung up before I could reply. I didn't have time to mourn my parents or Sean. I had to protect myself and my baby. After a deep breath, I jumped. I closed my eyes and reached for the nearest branch. I slammed into the trunk of the tree and slid down a ways before I was able to get a good enough grip to pull myself up. Once I was sitting on a branch, I looked down. It was less than a ten foot drop, but I wasn't ready for it yet.

"Miss? Are you okay?"

His voice startled me at first. When I looked down and saw that the man was wearing a police uniform, I felt calmer immediately.

***

I woke up just as I was jumping toward the police officer in my dream. And just like the last three nights, I was covered in sweat and could still feel tears on my cheeks.

Fed up with the nightmare, I decided not to go back to sleep. It was almost five in the morning; what better time to start my day?

After a long, much-needed shower, I got dressed and hopped into the Jeep. Without knowing exactly where I was going, I drove. I drove into the small town that I would be calling my home for the time being.

First thing's first: breakfast. A small café across the street from a truck stop was the first place I saw. I sat at a table and looked over the menu while trying to ignore the judgmental stares I was getting from two older men drinking coffee in the corner.

"Y'all going to introduce yourselves, or just keep starin'?" I heard an elderly woman ask. I looked up and saw that she was making her way to my table.

"What'll it be sweetheart?" she asked. I didn't miss the genuine smile on her face.

"I'll take two pieces of toast and a banana, please. Diet Coke to drink."

"Let's try that again, hun. Let me remind you that you're eating for two. And I will not be serving you caffeine until the day you come in with that baby on your hip."

"Uhh, waffles?" I asked.

She nodded her head and continued to look at me expectantly.

"Waffles and chocolate milk?"

"Waffles, chocolate milk, and that banana. Comin' right up," she said with a smile.

I smiled back at her and I was pretty certain it was the first real smile I'd worn in months. She was back with a tall glass of chocolate milk in less than a minute. The two men who had been staring at me walked out the door at the same time as she sat across from me.

"Don't you worry about them. They can't function in a regular society until their coffee has kicked in," she said with a wink.

I laughed at her comment before taking a sip of my chocolate milk.

"So what's your story? I know you're not from here. Those purple streaks in your hair are a dead giveaway."

"Oh, uh, I'm Payton. I moved here from, uh, Oklahoma. I just got in last night actually," I answered as casually as I could.

"Oklahoma? You're not the Parishs' niece are ya? I heard through the grapevine she was coming here for the summer."

"No, I don't know any Parishs', and I'll be here for more than just the summer."

"Well, I'm Gretta. I own this place and I'm here to chat any time ya like."

I nodded as she went to the back to get my breakfast.

After eating and using the facilities I asked Gretta where I could find some things for my bedroom. She pointed me in the direction of a boutique in the middle of town.

I parked the Jeep on the curb right out front of the small store. They had everything from rugs and lamps to bedframes and computer desks. This was the perfect place for me to find a few things that would make my house feel more like a home.

I grabbed a light blue bedspread and a set of lime green sheets. I tossed a couple of navy blue throw pillows onto the counter and let the woman at the register know I wanted those as well. An hour and a few hundred dollars later, I was heading back to my house with a Jeep full of home décor.

I hung a painting of sunflowers in my bedroom and put a green and grey striped rug beside the bed. I put the navy blue pillows on each end of the couch and laid a cream colored rug in the center of the living room.

Once I finished making the bed, I flopped down onto it. It was much more comfortable than the couch and it didn't take me long to start dozing off.

I'm not sure how long I had been asleep when the doorbell rang. I sat up quickly and opened the top drawer of the dresser. The taser that one of the agents had given me before I got on the plane was tucked behind a pile of my socks. I gripped it tightly in my shaking hand as I went to see who was at the door.

My racing heart slowed when I saw a UPS guy through the small peephole. I tucked the taser in the back of my shorts and opened the door.

"I've got a package for Payton Scott," the guy said.

"Uh, that's me."

"Sign here, please."

I signed where he instructed and took the yellow package from his hand before shutting the door. I went to the kitchen and used a knife to cut the packing tape off of the box. Inside was an Alabama phonebook with a folded piece of paper taped to the front:

Payton,

Use the phonebook to find a doctor for you and the baby ASAP.

Your savings account has been transferred to the local bank. Here is the key to your safety deposit box.

Find a job and make friends.

There was no signature on the note, but I knew it had to be from one of the agents in California. Nobody else knew my address, for starters, and they are the only people who would need to tell me the status of my savings account. Even though I was uncertain exactly who had sent the phonebook and note, it felt good to know that somebody was still looking out for me. The real me. Haley.

Gavin

"Sparks! My office! NOW!" my captain called over the intercom.

I knew what he wanted, and I knew I was going to get an earful as soon as I walked in there. Ignoring the mocking looks from my co-workers, I stood tall as I walked into his office and shut the door behind me.

"I'm not authorizing this," he snapped, slamming my transfer request down on his desk.

"Sir, with all due respect, I will be transferring with or without your help," I replied calmly.

"Alabama? Gavin, have you even thought this through? Nobody is supposed to know where she is! If you go there you will never be able to see your friends and family again. You can't invite them to visit and risk blowing her cover."

"Sir, we both know I don't have family, and the closest thing I have to a friend is you. No offense, but I think I can handle not seeing you again for a while," I smirked.

Rubbing his hands over his face, he asked, "You really want to give up everything for some pregnant girl with purple hair? She's a nobody, Sparks. You saved her and got her out of the life she was stuck in. You've done your part, now let it go."

My fists clenched at my sides and I forced myself to take a calming breath before opening my mouth again.

"She's not a 'nobody,' Sam. She *has* nobody! This isn't a negotiation. If you refuse to grant my transfer I will apply for the job the old fashioned way. Make your choice because I made mine the day you drove her to the airport."

Shaking his head, he leaned over and signed the paper. He handed my approved transfer request to me and I left without another word. For good.

I called the chief in Birmingham and let him know the good news. He told me my office would be ready in two weeks. The conversation ended quickly, which I was thankful for, because I had a lot to do before my flight the following afternoon.

I sped to my apartment and paid the landlord my last month of rent. Luckily, my new place in Birmingham was fully furnished, so I just had to pack my clothes and bathroom supplies and then I was good to go.

I forced myself to go to sleep right after dinner and a shower. I knew the chances of me seeing her soon were slim. If I just showed up at her door, it would terrify her, no doubt. But that didn't stop me from thinking about her constantly. Her dark brown hair matched her eyes perfectly. The streaks of purple in her hair and the feather tattoo on the inside of her ankle were just marks of being raised in L.A.

Despite what Sam thinks of her, she graduated college with a degree in marketing, and she chose to keep her baby even after she knew she would be doing it alone. That's not my definition of a "nobody."

My plane landed in Birmingham early the following morning. I took a cab to my new apartment complex and unpacked the one suitcase I had. Once everything was put away, I changed into some gym clothes. The fitness center the apartment complex offered was almost as nice as the one I'd had in LA. It was more than what I needed to sweat out the stress that came with my job.

After a quick workout and shower I called the chief to check in. I'd sent him money last week so he could get me a vehicle ready for when I arrived. He agreed to pick me up and show me around during his lunch break.

"Gavin Sparks. Good to see you again, man."

"Good to see you, too, Chief Jackson," I said while shaking his hand.

"If you call me Chief instead of Daniel one more time, you're getting a pay cut. We're friends here. Act like it."

"Yes, sir. Daniel it is."

He shook his head and laughed as we got into the patrol car he had picked me up in.

"On the rare occasion you get called into the field, you'll be driving this car. You're other mode of transportation is at the office," he said with a grin.

Daniel was about five years older than me. I had come to talk to him a couple of weeks ago while I was dropping the Jeep off at Payton's.

He was the chief of the drug trafficking department in Birmingham. They were starting a new undercover unit, and I was going to be the guy over that unit. I would be in an office setting the majority of the time, while my guys were in the field. I would have to get used to the change of pace, but I assumed the increase in pay would help with that.

"Hope you like black," Daniel muttered as we pulled up to the building both of our offices were in.

"Come again?"

"I said, 'I hope you like black.' Because the black one is yours," he said pointing to something outside my window.

I turned around to see what it was he was pointing at. It was a black Dodge truck.

"No shit? The money I sent you covered that?"

"Nah, but your Christmas bonus took care of the rest."

"Man, remind me to let you be responsible for my vehicle shopping from now on," I said, slapping him on the shoulder.

"Well, here are the keys. I'd take you inside, but your office still isn't ready. Enjoy your two weeks off. I'll be in touch."

After saying goodbye to Daniel and promising to relax during the next two weeks, I jumped into my new truck. It was a thirty-five minute drive to the small town where Payton lived, and I planned on spending a lot of time there over the next two weeks.

Payton

It had been a week since I'd gone to the bank and opened the safety deposit box. One week since I'd seen the fake birth certificate, immunization records, college diploma, and resume. It was hard to take it all in. My life back in L.A. could never be talked about and I could never go back there. The rest of my life would be fake. I would be pretending to be somebody I wasn't for the next eighty-something years.

I spent three days wallowing. The next two days were spent being angry at everyone. *How dare they let my life turn into this?* Yesterday, however, was a day of acceptance. Today was the day I'd start pretending to be Payton Scott from Oklahoma. Date of birth, November 3, 1991. My reason for moving to Alabama wasn't a total lie. I planned on telling people I was here for a fresh start. I'd just leave the part about it not being my choice out of the story.

To complete my day of pretending, I had a hair appointment. I couldn't live in this tiny, southern town and expect to fit in with purple streaks in my hair.

"What are we doin' today?" the girl with platinum blonde hair asked as she tugged at my hair.

"I want the purple out. So I guess just dye all of it a darker brown," I said cautiously.

"Aw, I like the purple. I've never been brave enough to try it."

"It's been fun, but I need my hair to be more subtle."

"Understood. How would you feel about a dark brown with a red hue to it? The color looks so shiny in the light, and you have the perfect skin tone for it."

"Sure. That will work," I shrugged.

She clapped her hands together and made quick work of mixing the color together and painting it on my shoulder length hair. She made small talk while she was working. Her name was Kate, and she was a few months younger than me. She had been doing hair for two years now and she waitressed at a steakhouse on the weekends.

"Where do you work?" she asked.

"Uh, I don't have a job yet. I just moved here."

"Oh, well, the steakhouse is hiring a waitress. I could put in a good word for you if you're interested?"

"Thanks. I'll think about it and let you know."

After my hair was finished, I paid Kate and tipped her well. She was right about the color going well with my skin tone. It was a relief to know that I would have a decent hair stylist while living here.

Before heading home I stopped by the steakhouse Kate had talked about. I went in to get some dinner and to see what the place was like. The inside was decorated in western style décor. I didn't have to wait to be seated, which made sense because it was barely 4pm. The dinner crowd wouldn't be showing up for a couple of hours, I assumed.

The waitress who took my order was young. She couldn't have been older than twenty. She was sweet and attentive.

"Have you been working here long?" I asked her.

"Somethin' like that. My parents own it," she smirked.

"Oh, do you know if they are needing any extra help?"

"Are you askin' for yourself?"

I nodded.

"We need a lunchtime server. Six days a week. The pay sucks, but the tips are usually good. Want an application?"

"I'd love one," I answered.

I filled out the application while I ate my chicken strips. I handed it back to the waitress when she brought me the bill.

"You can come in Saturday around ten for an official interview. I'll let my mom know that you would be a good fit," she said with a wink.

"Thanks! And keep the change!" I called to her before leaving.

At home, I showered and slipped on some yoga pants and a tank top. I searched the TV for a good movie to watch but didn't have much luck, so I settled on the Lifetime channel just to pass the time while the sun went down. My first OB appointment was tomorrow morning. I was trying not to think about it or my nerves would get the best of me.

***

"Come on, Hales. I know something is going on with you. Spill it," Sean ordered.

"I'm pregnant, Sean. I've taken six different tests. It's the real deal."

I watched his eyes grow to twice their normal size as he looked at my stomach. The second he looked into my eyes, I knew. He didn't want us.

"Shit! Haley, you said you were on the pill!"

"I've been on the pill since I was sixteen. It's not one hundred percent, though; you know that."

"Get an abortion. That's one hundred percent effective," he snapped.

My hands instinctively went to my flat stomach. I stared at Sean a moment longer, waiting for him to realize what he'd just said and take it back. He stared back at me with hard, unforgiving eyes.

"I'm not doing that, Sean," I whispered.

The look on his face was pure anger. "Whatever you do, you're doing it on your own. I'm not being a dad, Haley. You've known that from the beginning."

I turned away from him so he wouldn't see the tears pooling in my eyes. I heard the front door to our apartment slam shut and I knew he was gone. I was sure he wouldn't be coming back soon, but I wasn't going to be here when he did. I packed all of my things and went to my parent's house.

"You're going to be okay, sweetheart. Your father and I will help you. You're going to be a great mother, and I'm going to be a grandmother!"

My mom's excitement over the baby was contagious, and her promise to help was a big relief. I went to sleep happy that night.

"Haley? Haley, can you hear me? Why aren't you helping us, Haley? You are the only one that can stop them, Haley. We are your parents! Why aren't you saving us?"

***

I jolted upright and frantically looked around for my mother. Her cries had been so clear in my dream. They sounded so real. As if she were standing right next me.

My hands were trembling and it took me a moment to catch my breath. Once I had calmed down a little I remembered falling asleep on the couch. I glanced at the clock on the wall. It wasn't even 6am.

I knew trying to sleep after that dream was pointless, so I took a long shower. I tried to push the memories of the dream out of my mind, but I knew I'd be having the same dream again soon.

I stopped at Gretta's café for breakfast before going to my OB appointment. She brought a glass of chocolate milk to my table without even asking.

"Good morning, Payton. I like your new hair color. It suits you well."

"Thanks, Gretta. I guess I just needed a little more change in my life."

"Ah, I understand. So, what are you doing out and about so early this morning?" she asked as she sat in the chair across from me.

"I've got an appointment to check on the baby," I said with a nervous smile.

"Oh! How exciting!"

"I'm more nervous than excited. I know I should have gone to the doctor before now. But I've had so much going on lately…" I trailed off.

"I'm sure everything will be fine. We'd bettered cut the chitchat or you won't have time to eat before you go. What'll it be today?"

"Waffles and a banana, please."

Gretta nodded at me before returning to the kitchen to place my order. I hoped she was right about my appointment. I hoped everything was going to be fine.

"You better be back in soon to let me know what the doc tells ya," Gretta said as I was getting up to leave.

"I'll see you soon, Gretta," I promised her.

I sat in the cold waiting room at the doctor's office for over twenty minutes before a nurse called my name. My fake name.

After getting my height and weight we went into an exam room. We reviewed my fake immunization list and the contact information for my fake family doctor.

"Is this your first pregnancy?" the nurse asked without looking up from her clipboard.

"Yes."

"And was it a planned pregnancy?"

"No."

"Uh-huh. And is the baby's father still in the picture?"

"No."

She looked up at me for a brief second before rattling off twenty-something more questions.

"The doctor will be in shortly," she told me before leaving the room.

Less than ten minutes later a woman close to my mom's age walked in.

"Hello, Payton. I'm Dr. Grey. It's nice to meet you."

I shook her hand and forced a smile.

"So, this is your first appointment for this pregnancy, correct?"

"Yes.

"Well, I am so glad you came in today," she said with a sincere looking smile. "Have you been taking any prenatal vitamins, Payton?"

"No. But I have stopped drinking caffeine."

"Great. That's a healthy choice for you and your baby. Not all expectant mothers take prenatal vitamins, but I highly recommend them. I will write you a prescription for them before you leave today.

"Okay," I nodded.

"I see here that the baby's father will not be present during your pregnancy. Do you have any friends or family who are planning to be with you during delivery?"

"No," I answered quietly. "It's just me."

She looked at me sympathetically for a moment before changing the subject.

"Well then, I think we've wasted enough time. How about we see that baby?"

"Okay," I said nervously.

The nurse instructed me to lie back and lift my shirt over my stomach.

"This will feel a little cold at first, Payton," Dr. Grey said.

I nodded as she squirted some clear gel onto my stomach below my belly button. After a few loud, weird noises, a constant *whoosh, whoosh, whoosh* sound came from the machine.

"Do you hear that? That is the baby's heart beat," Dr. Grey said.

"Why does it sound like that? Is something wrong?" I asked nervously.

"Oh, no, honey. Everything sounds great. If you look at the monitor I can show you the heart beating."

I swallowed hard before focusing my attention onto the computer screen. She pointed her finger to the middle of the screen where something grey was blinking in sync with the *whooshing* sound.

"There it is, Payton. That's your baby."

Tears started running down my face as I stared at the screen.

"Judging by the baby's size, you are about sixteen weeks along. We should be able to determine the gender next month if you would like."

"Really? You can tell that soon?"

"In most cases, yes."

All I could do was nod so she would know I was listening.

"Everything seems to be progressing just fine, Payton. Start taking your prenatal vitamins and I'll see you again in four weeks. Don't hesitate to call with any questions," Dr. Grey said before shaking my hand and leaving the room.

The nurse wiped the gel off of my stomach and handed me a prescription for the vitamins I had to pick up. I scheduled my next appointment at the front desk and asked the receptionist where the closest pharmacy was. She gave me simple directions and let me know that it would only take them a few minutes to have it ready. I thanked her and was on my way, feeling more relaxed now that I knew everything was going fine.

Gavin

I didn't go back to Birmingham as I'd planned. After I saw Payton at that restaurant that night, I couldn't make myself leave town. I was sitting in the booth behind her, so I knew she didn't see me. I also knew she wouldn't have recognized me even if she had.

I recognized her as soon as she walked in. The purple streaks were no longer in her hair and her belly was starting to look more like a baby bump, but it was her. I wanted to go to her when I saw her sit at a table alone, but I resisted. I watched her pick at her food while she filled out a job application. After she left, I asked the waitress if they were going to hire her. She told me that her parents did all the hiring, but she was pretty certain they would like her. I would definitely be eating there more often.

I drove by her place after leaving the steakhouse to make sure she had made it home safely. That's the reason I was going with, anyway. Honestly, I spent every second of my spare time trying to think of places I could "accidentally" bump into her. All I had to go on was her interview at the restaurant tomorrow morning. I got a hotel room for the night and planned on seeing her in the morning.

I stopped at a small drug store to get some deodorant, a toothbrush, and toothpaste. I asked the woman at the register where I could find everything, and she pointed me in the direction of aisle eight. I was making my way through the aisles when I heard a lot of something fall to the floor. I took two steps back to look down aisle five, and there she was. She was using the shelves as a ladder, trying to reach something on the top shelf. In the process, she had knocked about ten bottles of bubble bath to the ground.

"Ma'am, do you need some help?" I asked, trying to hide my grin.

"Uh, yeah, please?" she blushed as she looked down at the floor. Her feet were on the third shelf and she was hanging on to the edge of the top shelf for dear life.

"I'm going to help you down, okay?"

She nodded her approval and I put my hands on her hips. Her frame was so tiny, I felt like I was going to break her. I silently counted to three before lifting her off and away from the shelves and gently setting her down.

"Thanks," she mumbled before bending down to pick up the bottles on the floor.

I squatted down to her level. "Did you need help reaching something?"

"Forget it. I can get it later," she huffed.

I stood and looked at the top shelf to see what she could have been going after. I grabbed a bottle of lavender scented baby lotion without even straightening my arm fully.

"Is this what you wanted?" I asked, grinning.

"Yes, thank you," she said sheepishly.

"You know, it doesn't look like you're going to be needing that for a few more months," I said, gesturing toward her barely there baby bump.

"Oh, it's for me. I read an article today at the doctor's office that said if you use the same kind of soap and lotion while you're pregnant that you plan to use on the baby, then he or she will feel more comfortable taking baths."

So, she had found a doctor. Thank God. She was looking at me expectantly and I realized

I hadn't said anything back to her. I turned around and grabbed a bottle of baby soap that was also lavender scented and held it out to her.

"So, you need this too, right?"

"Yes, thanks," she said with a small smile that had my heart rate picking up speed.

"Payton Scott, your prescription is ready," a man's voice came over the speakers.

"Oh, that's me. Thanks again for the help," she said over her shoulder as she started walking away.

"Anytime, Payton," I called.

She waved over her shoulder without turning around. Her Jeep wasn't in the parking lot by the time I got outside, but I didn't let it bring down my mood. I knew I would be seeing her again tomorrow.

I hate sleeping in hotels. The beds are always uncomfortable and the rooms are either too hot or ice cold. I gave up trying to get a good night's sleep around 5am. I spent a couple of hours watching *SportsCenter* before taking a shower. I had no choice but to put the same clothes back on when I got out. I grabbed my things and checked out of the hotel before 8am.

I was driving around, trying to pass the time, when I saw her Jeep parked across the street from a truck stop. It looked like some sort of diner. Unable to stop myself, I pulled into the parking lot and turned off my truck. I was beginning to love the idea of her being in a small town. I would have never seen her again if they'd moved her to Birmingham like they'd originally planned.

"So, are ya hoping for a boy or girl?" I heard an older woman ask when I walked through the door. I looked to my left and saw her sitting at a table and the older woman was sitting across from her. Neither of them had heard me walk in, so I stood still as I waited to hear her answer.

"Well, everybody always says they just want a healthy baby. Which is what I want, of course. But, if I were able to choose, I would choose a girl. I can't raise a boy by myself; I don't know the first thing about little boys," she said with a laugh. The woman started saying something to her that I couldn't hear because I was too busy walking right up to their table.

"Wow, this really is a small town, huh?" I asked. The woman jumped out of her seat after realizing she had another customer.

"Sorry, I didn't even hear ya come in. Go ahead and sit wherever ya like. Would ya like some coffee?"

"Thank you, ma'am, but I'll just have a water."

"I'll be right back with a menu," she said before walking away.

Payton was still staring at me when I turned back to her.

"Can I join you?" I asked.

Her eyebrows shot up at my question, but she nodded her approval.

"It's Payton, right?" I asked her.

Another nod.

"Well, Payton, I'm Gavin. Gavin Sparks."

"Sorry, but are you wearing the same shirt you wore yesterday?" she whispered.

I couldn't help but laugh. "Yes, I am. I live in Birmingham and ended up having to stay in a hotel last night. I didn't have a change of clothes with me, but I did shower. I swear."

She cocked an eyebrow at me as she considered my story.

"What are you doing here if you live in Birmingham? I'm sure it's way more interesting there."

"Well, I think it's been pretty interesting here, so far," I said with a wink. She looked down at her plate, but not before I saw the blush creep into her cheeks.

"Oh, y'all know each other?" the older woman asked as she sat my water on the table.

"We're getting to know each other," I said before Payton could answer her. "I'm Gavin Sparks. It's nice to meet you," I said as I extended my hand to her.

"Well, it is very nice to meet you too, Gavin. I'm Gretta Johnson. I own this ol' place."

"What do you suggest for breakfast, Gretta?"

"This girl won't try nothin' but the waffles. But the omelets are delicious," she said with a smile.

"That sounds perfect," I told her. She nodded and walked back to the kitchen.

"She seems nice," I said to Payton so she would finally look up at me again.

"She's great. She's the closest thing I have to a friend here."

"Haven't lived here long?" I asked, even though I knew the answer.

"Seems like I've been here a lot longer than I really have," she says quietly. I hated that she hated it here, and I hated that she was obviously lonely.

"Surely you have friends at work, don't you?"

"I don't have a job yet. I've actually got an interview today, in about twenty minutes. I should probably go." She started gulping down her chocolate milk and standing up at the same time. She left cash on the table and was walking to the door before I had time to say anything.

"I'll see you around then," I said before she opened the door.

"Probably not, Gavin. Have fun in Birmingham."

And then she was out the door.

I stayed and chatted with Gretta while I ate my omelet. I could see why Payton liked her so much. I knew it would be stalkerish if I went to the steakhouse to see her again, so I reluctantly made the drive back to Birmingham. I would be starting work on Monday, and I was certain I wouldn't be seeing Payton often, and that thought frustrated me.

Payton

That morning I woke up and felt rested for the first time in over a month. I practically skipped to the calendar hanging on my fridge and marked off the square in which I had written, *17 weeks*, and *First day of work*. I hadn't had any nightmares last night and had gone to bed happy. I'd found a doctor for me and the baby and gotten a job. Now, I just needed to make some friends at my job and maybe I would start feeling like I belonged here.

I was brushing my teeth when I felt the fluttering feeling in my stomach. It had been happening more frequently since the first time I felt it last Saturday. I had thought I was just nervous about my interview or that I was getting butterflies from the amazingly hot guy who ate breakfast with me. But it kept happening on Sunday and I realized that it was my baby. The little thing was flipping and flopping more often than not now, and it was an amazing feeling.

The owners of the steakhouse were Lisa and Craig, and their daughter's name was Hannah. My interview was short and sweet. They asked if I had any experience in waitressing, and I had to lie and say "no" because it wasn't on my fake resume. I promised them I was a fast learner and that I could work any hours they needed me to. They hired me on the spot but didn't need me to come in until the following Tuesday.

I showered and took the time to curl my hair and slip a head band on to keep my hair out of my face. I used a little mascara but wanted to keep my makeup natural.

I was only working until 3pm today. Lisa wanted me to get a feel for things on the lunch shift. She said I would be ready for the dinner rush by the weekend. I wasn't worried. I had been a waitress at a restaurant in L.A. throughout college.

I liked that the dress code was casual. I wore skinny jeans, a black fitted shirt, and black Converse. I knew my feet were going to be killing me after my shift, but I couldn't find any shoes that I liked at the local stores. Gretta suggested I go to Birmingham to do my shopping, but I didn't want to go alone.

When I got to the restaurant, Kate and Hannah were rolling silverware at a table in the back.

"Hey, Payton! I'm so glad you got the job," Kate said.

"I thought you only worked on weekends?" I asked her.

"I do. But I took this week off at the salon so I could help Hannah show you the ropes."

"Oh, well, I appreciate it."

"No problem. Come to the back and I'll show you around before the nooners start coming in."

"Nooners?" I asked, confused.

"Oh, that's just what we call the people that come in during the lunch rush," Hannah explained.

"Got it."

My shift went by surprisingly quickly. Once Kate saw that I knew what I was doing, she let me take over half of her tables. We had all the tables cleared and had swept and mopped the dining area before 3pm. Craig cashed me and Kate out, but Hannah had to work the split.

"See you at five!" Kate called to Hannah as we were walking out the back door.

"So, you look like you know what you're doing in there. Want to tell me why you told Lisa and Craig you didn't have any experience?" Kate asked.

"Uh, I didn't want them to expect me to be better than I am and then be disappointed," I lied.

"Hmm, good point."

"I'll see you tomorrow," I said as I got into my Jeep.

Kate waved as I pulled away.

When I turned down my road I saw a truck parked in my driveway. Fear shot through me, but I didn't stop driving. I took a deep breath and pulled into my driveway. *Nobody knows where you are; it's probably just a neighbor*, I said to myself.

I was wrong.

I got out of my Jeep slowly and waited for the driver of the truck to step out. A tall man with shaggy black hair got out with his back to me. When he turned around my entire body went stiff.

"Surprised to see me, Hales?" he asked with a smile on his face.

"What are you doing here, Tyler?"

"You know, I thought I was going crazy when I saw you at that diner yesterday. But when I saw you today at the restaurant and heard your voice, I knew it was you."

He started walking toward me and I started backing up.

"What do you want from me?" I asked with a shaky voice.

"Stop acting like you don't know why I've spent the last month looking for you!" he snapped. He came even closer now. I could see that his eyes were bloodshot and had dark rings around them. It was obvious that he was using again.

"I'm not acting, Tyler. I don't know what you want."

"Sean is dead. And his blood is on your hands. The minute you walked out of his life and chose that baby over him, you put a target on his head."

"Tyler, you're confused. I didn't have anything to do with Sean's murder. The same people tried to kill me, too," my voice broke at the end. I was trying to keep it together in front of him, but I wasn't going to last much longer.

"Clearly, you are the one that's confused, Haley. I killed Sean. They made me do it. And now, I'm here to do what the other guys couldn't. Unless you want to pay."

My heart was pounding in my chest. Tyler had been Sean's best friend since middle school. If he'd killed Sean, I know he wouldn't hesitate to kill me.

"How much do you want?" I whispered.

"Well, I know your parents left you a pretty penny. So, why don't you tell me how much you've got."

"They didn't leave me as much as you think," I lied. "I've got thirty thousand in the bank. Come inside. I will write you a check."

I was trying to come across as confident and sure of everything I was doing, when really, I was terrified.

"I'll take thirty grand for now. When I come back you'd better have double."

I didn't say anything as I unlocked the door to my house. I smelled the alcohol on his breath once we got inside.

"My checkbook is in the back room. I'll be just a second." I turned and tried to walk to my bedroom, but he grabbed me by the elbow and jerked me back to him. A whimper escaped my lips at the pain of his grip on my arm.

"You still think I'm stupid don't you, Hales?"

The tears were falling freely down my cheeks now and I couldn't catch my breath to speak. I shook my head, but I wasn't quick enough. His fist connected with the side of my head a second later.

I knew my eyes were open, but all I could see was black. I blinked harder and harder until my vision finally came back. Tyler was leaning over on the counter breathing hard. I stared at his trembling body for a minute before I realized what was wrong with him. He was having withdrawals from whatever he was hooked on now. I heard him start to make gagging noises and I knew I had time. I turned and sprinted to my bedroom. I grabbed the taser out of my dresser and started making my way back down the hallway. When I came into the kitchen,

Tyler was right where I'd left him. There was puke running off the counter onto my floor. I counted to three in my head, took a deep breath, and held the taser to his neck. When I knew it was in a good spot, I pressed the button and held it. It felt like an hour passed by before he collapsed onto the floor.

When I was certain he was unconscious, the reality of what was happening hit me. I fell to my knees and started sobbing. I don't know how much time had passed, but when I saw Tyler's foot twitch I pulled myself together.

I dug the temporary phone out of the junk drawer in my kitchen and powered it on. The number to the agent in L.A. was written in Sharpie on the back. I remember the captain handing it to me before he dropped me off at the airport.

"Sparks," the male voice answered.

Gavin

Thank God I was on my way to her house when she called. I was only twenty minutes away, but I was going to make it in ten. I called Sam on the way to fill him in.

"Ah, Sparks. Ready to come back so soon?" he asked.

"Hardly. Want to tell me how the hell Tyler Donelli found Haley Golds?"

"What are you talking about?" he snapped. Now I knew I had his attention.

"She just called me off of her emergency phone. Tyler Donelli was working with Sean Sanford. She said he threatened to kill her and she tased him. I'm on my way there now."

"How the fuck did this happen?" he yelled.

"That's what I want to know. Who's supposed to be tailing him?"

"I'll handle it, Sparks. Take Donelli back to Birmingham with you. I will be there to escort him to his cell tomorrow morning."

I hung up and called one of my guys in Birmingham. I explained that I was working on an old case and that I needed a holding cell for Donelli.

I pulled into her driveway and grabbed a set of handcuffs out of my glove box.

I opened the front door without knocking and saw her sitting on the couch with her knees pulled tight to her chest. I rushed over and knelt in front of her. Her eyes weren't focused and her head was slightly swaying side to side.

"You have a concussion. I'm calling the ambulance," I told her.

After I gave the address to the first responders, I took a good look at the unconscious body in her kitchen floor. He was out cold, but I cuffed him anyway. I went out to the garage and found some duct tape to wrap around his ankles. That should hold him for the drive.

I sat next to Payton until the ambulance arrived. She didn't say anything, but she kept staring at me. I knew she recognized me, but I hoped she wouldn't remember it tomorrow.

The EMTs came inside to check her vitals. They determined that she needed to go to the hospital to be checked out more thoroughly because of the baby. I carried her to the ambulance and watched them drive away. When I could no longer see the flashing lights, I went through Donelli's truck. There was a gun in the glove box and an empty bag on the passenger seat. The white powdery residue indicated that the bag had contained cocaine at one point. Donelli didn't have any identification on him or in his truck. I notice the plates on the truck were from Nebraska, so I assumed it was stolen.

I called the local sheriff's office to have the truck impounded before loading Donelli into my backseat. He remained unconscious until I parked the truck. He started groaning and grunting when I opened the door to get him out.

"Where am I?" he croaked.

"On your way to a cell," I said matter-of-factly.

"What the fuck happened?"

"Well, I'd say, you messed with the wrong girl."

"Hales? She turned me in? We're like family! Fucking bitch!"

What little control I had left snapped the second he called her a bitch. I jerked him out of the truck and slammed him against the brick wall of the building. My forearm was pressed against his throat and my face was barely an inch away from his.

"You go near her again and you will wake up in hell. Consider yourself lucky to be able to see the inside of a cell today."

"I'll take it from here, man," someone said from behind me.

I turned to see Daniel standing behind me. I let go of Donelli and let him walk inside with the chief. I wanted to go back to check on Payton, but I had a lot of explaining to do first. I could tell the chief was pissed, but I knew he would understand.

I waited by my truck for half an hour before Daniel came back outside.

"Chief, I can explain," I started.

"No need. Your captain called. He sent me the file on Haley Golds."

"He did?" I asked, shocked.

"I don't know why you gave it all up to keep an eye on her, but you and I both know what could have happened tonight if you hadn't have been so close."

"I'm trying not to think about the possibilities," I said through gritted teeth.

"Go home. I don't want you leaving town until this piece of trash is out of my jail. Understood?"

"Yes, sir," I nodded.

I went home like I'd promised, but I was up all night worrying about Payton. I knew she would be fine once her head stopped aching. The thing that had me worried was that now she knew I was a cop. It wouldn't be long before she started putting everything together, and I worried she'd think I was there for the wrong reasons.

Sam was waiting at the jail for me the next morning.

"Morning, Captain."

"Good morning, Sparks. I guess I owe you an apology," he said, squeezing the back of his neck.

"Don't worry about it, sir. I'm confident you and your guys won't let anything like this happen again," I said with a cocked brow.

He nodded.

We agreed to question Donelli together. The little bitch started spilling his guts within the first five minutes. He'd been shunned by his crowd because he wouldn't stop using the product. Sean and Tyler worked for one of the biggest drug dealers in California. Haley's brother Josh had been in on it, too, before he was killed. Sam had a couple of leads suggesting that Haley's parents were part of the group, but there was never enough proof to collar them.

"I was just looking for my next hit. I saw her walk into some diner downtown. At first, I thought there was no way that could be Hales. Vincent said he'd finished her off along with her parents," Donelli told us.

"Why were you going to kill her? She doesn't have any drugs to give you," Sam said.

"I know that, but her parents were loaded. I knew she would give me money if I threatened her and that baby."

"We're done here," I cut him off.

"Take him to my cruiser out back," Sam told one of the deputies before turning to me. "So, they all think Haley Golds is dead. Donelli is too fried; nobody would believe him if he told them otherwise. I don't think it's a good idea to relocate her right now. She's just getting comfortable."

I blew out a breath I hadn't realized I was holding. Sam was right. We couldn't make her run for the rest of her life.

"I'll talk to her. She can decide what she wants to do," I told him.

"She knows you're the one that saved her then?"

I shook my head. "She saved herself, Sam."

Payton

The nurses at the hospital didn't tell me much when I woke up. They said I'd been hit in the head with something and had a concussion. They offered me pain medication, but I refused. After they'd given me fluids through an IV, I was free to go.

I made up a story about being clumsy and slipping in the shower to explain the bruise on the left side of my face. Kate and Hannah accepted my story, but they didn't look convinced. A few customers asked me about it, but none of them pressed for information.

It was Saturday night and it seemed like the whole town wanted to eat at the steakhouse. My feet were killing me and I was starting to get a headache, but there were still three hours until closing.

"The guy sitting in my section is asking for you," Hannah told me.

"What? Who is it?" I tried not to sound as scared as I felt. For all I knew Tyler had gone back and told all of L.A. where to find me.

"Hot Stuff, over there in the corner booth," she said, putting her hand over her heart and letting out an exaggerated sigh. I rolled my eyes at her before turning around to see Gavin Sparks sitting in the booth.

He might be hot, but now I knew he was a liar. He didn't bother telling me he was a cop either time we met. When I called the number on the back of my emergency phone, I hadn't realized that the Sparks that answered was Gavin Sparks. Even when he showed up and handcuffed Tyler, I still thought he just happened to be in the right place at the right time.

After I came to my senses in the hospital, I put it all together. The captain from L.A. had to have recruited him to keep an eye on me. That has to be how he knew the way to my house. The bad news for him is that I'm not interested in being babysat for the rest of my life.

I was still staring at him when he looked up and our eyes met. I gave him my best glare before walking in the opposite direction to check on the tables in my section.

"He's all yours," I told Hannah as I walked away.

Gavin stayed for almost two hours.

"Guess lover boy finally took the hint, huh?" Hannah joked after he left.

"Perfect timing. Let's clean up and get out of here. My feet are killing me," I groaned.

"That's the best idea I've heard all night," she smirked.

We had everything cleaned and ready for the next day in no time. Hannah practically ran out the door to her car. I, on the other hand, hobbled slowly to the Jeep on my aching feet.

As soon as I got home I started running the water for a hot bath. I had the next two days off. I would definitely be spending one of those days getting new shoes.

I was just stepping into the tub when my doorbell rang. I let out a frustrated sigh and put on my robe. I grabbed the taser out of my dresser before going to the door because I wasn't taking any chances.

I saw Gavin Sparks through the tiny peephole. He was wearing khaki shorts and a white t-shirt. The sleeve of tattoos on his right arm was on full display. I would have taken my time appreciating his looks, but he rang the doorbell again. Rolling my eyes, I slung the door open, making sure my taser was in plain sight.

Gavin raised his hands and took a step back. "Is that really necessary?" he asked, nodding toward the taser.

"Well, a man I barely know knows where I live when I'm positive I've never given him my address. So, you tell me."

"I'm here to explain, Payton. You don't need a weapon. I'm not going to hurt you," he promised, taking two steps closer.

"I know you won't hurt me, Gavin. You're a cop that's getting paid to babysit me."

"It's not like that. Yes, I'm a cop, but I'm not here to babysit you."

I took a step toward him and pushed the button on my taser as I stuck it to his stomach for half a second.

"You've got to be kidding me," he groaned after falling to his knees.

"Just for good measure," I said with a grin. "When you're ready to tell me who you really are, come inside."

A solid ten minutes passed before Gavin came inside to sit on the couch. He sat on the end opposite of me and gave me his best glare.

"If you ever tase me again I will revoke your taser privileges."

"Then how would I protect myself from guys like Tyler?" I asked, feigning innocence.

"You would have to have a bodyguard to replace the taser. That would be me, of course," he smirked.

"Fine, no more tasing," I promised.

Gavin smiled before standing up and pacing in front of me. I stared at him expectantly while he ran his fingers through his short brown hair.

"I have a proposition for you, Payton."

I cocked an eyebrow at him and waited for him to continue.

"First, you need to know that I'm not on the clock right now. I'm not here to babysit or because I have to be."

"Then why are you here, Gavin?"

"Well, I wanted to be here. But I've been having second thoughts since you tased me," he said, raising his eyebrows.

I covered my mouth as I laughed. "I put the taser away, I swear."

"When is your next day off?"

"Tomorrow. Why?"

"Great. I'm taking you to Birmingham so you can get some comfortable shoes for work. You probably need some maternity clothes, too, right?"

My mouth dropped open and I stood up off of the couch. "Do my clothes look too small, Gavin? A little too tight for your taste, huh?"

"Sit back down, hothead. Your clothes are fine, but you and I both know they won't fit for much longer," he said as he stared at where my robe was covering my stomach.

"Thanks for your concern, but I'm more than capable of taking myself shopping," I huffed as I sat back down on the couch. "Now, tell me about this proposition of yours."

He shook his head at my attitude and sat down next to me.

"The proposition is, get to know me. Then, and only then, will I tell you the real reason I'm here. Hell, I'll tell you anything you want to know. But not until you get to know me."

"And if I don't want to get to know you, then what? You'll just keep stalking me and coming to my rescue when I need it?"

He nodded and I started shaking my head at the same time.

"It doesn't look like people are beating down your front door offering you their friendship, Payton. Stop acting like this is a hard decision."

I crossed my arms over my chest and drew my eyebrows together. He was right. The closest thing I had to a friend was Gretta, and I wasn't about to ask her to spend the day shopping with me. If I were back in L.A. and this guy offered to spend the day with me, I would have jumped at the opportunity. That was when I knew who I was and what I wanted in life. Now, I was stuck pretending to be someone else, and I have no future plans outside of next week. If I agreed to get to know Gavin, I'd also be agreeing to lie to him from the get go.

"Fine, I'll be ready at 10."

"See you then, Payton," he said, walking himself to the door.

I drained my cold bath water and took a quick shower instead. I think I fell asleep before my head even hit the pillow.

***

"Daddy! Sean's dad is here!" I called.

"Hales, what have I told you about answering the door by yourself?" Dad scolded.

"You said not until I'm older. But I'm almost ten, Daddy."

"Wait until you're eleven, then we will talk about it," he said as he stroked my hair.

I watched Sean's dad, Chris, hand my dad a thick yellow envelope.

"Where's the rest, Chris?" Daddy asked him.

"It's mine. You won't be getting another cent from me or my family, Jason."

"Haley, go upstairs and check on your mother," Daddy ordered.

I hugged his waist and waved goodbye to Chris before turning to walk up the stairs. I stopped on the top step and strained my ears to hear the conversation downstairs.

"Jason, we want out. I don't want Sean to live this life."

"Sean will choose this path whether you expose him to it or not. Smart men don't turn down money. So, what does that make you, Chris?"

"I have nothing else to say on the matter."

"You have until midnight to get the rest of my money. If I don't get what I want, you won't be around to see the life your son will live," Daddy said before slamming the door in his face.

I started to walk back down the stairs. I was going to beg Daddy not to send Chris away like he had the others. I liked Chris, and Sean was my best friend.

"Chris is out," Daddy bit out.

I poked my head into his office and saw that he was already on his cell phone. I knew it was too late. I'd never see Chris again. I went to my room and cried until mom came to check on me.

"Hales, don't cry. Saying goodbye to old friends and making new friends is all part of life. You're going to have to get used to it, dear," she said as she rubbed my back while I sobbed into my pillow.

"I know, Mom, but I'll really miss Sean," I sniffed.

"Well, I will see if I can talk to your father. Maybe we can keep in touch with Sean."

"Thank you," I whispered.

I woke up with tears running down my cheeks. I got out of bed quickly and took a deep breath as I pushed the memory out my mind.

Gavin

I slept like shit. Hotel beds are the worst. I should have gone back to my place last night. I could have gotten up early and had plenty of time to get to Payton's, but I'd made up countless excuses to be closer to her.

I took a cold shower and stopped by Gretta's café to get a bagel and chocolate milk for Payton. I pulled into her driveway thirty minutes early.

"You like shopping so much you couldn't wait 'til ten?" she teased with her toothbrush still in her mouth and toothpaste on her lips.

"Something like that," I smirked before walking inside.

"I need ten more minutes," she called over her shoulder as she walked back to her bedroom.

"I was hoping you weren't planning on wearing that hoodie," I called back to her. I was lying, of course. I'd let her wear anything with no complaint.

Fifteen minutes later she came out of her room wearing a black tank top that hugged her baby bump and a pair of cut off jean shorts. Her hair was in loose curls that looked so soft I had to force myself not to reach out and run my fingers through them.

"Let's do this," she said with a grin as she slipped on her sunglasses.

I checked her door after she locked it. She rolled her eyes at me before walking to her Jeep.

"What are you doing? We're taking my truck."

"Let's just take mine. You can drive it," she said as she dangled her keys in front of my face.

"Okay, you win. Let me grab my stuff."

She was buckling her seatbelt when I knocked on her window. She rolled it down and I handed her the to-go cup filled with chocolate milk and the paper bag that had her bagel in it.

"Breakfast," I said before walking to the driver's side.

"Thanks. You didn't have to do that."

"Don't mention it."

Payton was quiet for most of the hour drive. We pulled up to the mall a little before 11am.

"Do you want to get lunch first?" I asked her.

"I just ate," she said with a cocked brow.

"Just making sure you're not hungry."

"I'm fine, Gavin. I will tell you when I get hungry, I promise."

I nodded and she smiled.

"Where should we go first?" she asked with excitement.

"To a shoe store. I never want to see you limping at work again."

"I never want to wear Converse to work a double again," she joked.

We went to three different shoe stores before she found a pair worth trying on. I watched as she slipped the tiny black Nike onto her foot. She stood up and paced in front of me, one foot with her flip-flop and the other with the new shoe candidate.

"What do you think?" she asked.

"Well, they look like every other pair of Nikes we've seen today," I joked. "How do they feel?"

"They're comfortable, and I like the black for work, but I like that purple pair for my days off."

I turned to look at the other pair she had pointed at and nodded my agreement. She asked the sales associate to bring her the right size and went to wait at the register. I grabbed her bags before she had the chance and carried them out of the store.

"I can carry those. They aren't even heavy," she insisted.

"I know you can carry them, Payton. How about lunch?"

"Fine," she said as she rolled her eyes.

After lunch, we spent the next three hours going into random stores. She bought some shirts and a pair of jeans. She refused to wear the maternity jeans because she wanted to have a real button holding up her jeans.

When it was obvious that she was getting tired, I started fake yawning.

"Are you tired?" she asked.

"Yeah, I didn't get much sleep," I told her.

"Neither did I. We can head back if you're ready."

Payton fell asleep ten minutes into the drive. It was almost six o'clock by the time we made it back to her place. I turned off the ignition and watched her sleep for a moment before waking her. I watched her chest move up and down with each breath, then moved down to her stomach. I wondered if she could feel the baby moving yet. I wondered if she was excited or scared, or if she had wanted any kids before this happened. I knew those questions would have to wait, but I hoped she would answer them someday.

"Payton, we're back," I said quietly. She opened her eyes and looked around before looking at me.

"Sorry I fell asleep," she muttered.

"Don't worry about it. You can take me to dinner next week to make it up to me."

"I'll think about it," she smiled.

I checked the lock on her door before getting into my truck. I made the drive to my place at a much faster pace. My bed was calling my name the second I walked into my apartment. I stripped down to my boxers and fell face first onto my pillow.

I was in that same position when my alarm went off the next morning. After a quick gym session, I got ready for work.

"What're you smiling about this mornin', boss?" Evan asked.

"Just happy to be here I guess," I lied.

"Whatever you say, man," he laughed. "So, Dino got some news on the Granger Boys. They're expecting a shipment around Thanksgiving. Dino says he'll be in deep until then and won't have much contact."

"Well, that gives us four months to prepare. I want everyone informed every step of the way. Keep me updated."

"Yes, sir," he said before walking out of my office.

Dino was my only agent undercover at the moment. He was working with a gang we called the Granger Boys. The Granger Boys were a group of guys who worked for Rick Granger. He had a laundry list of priors but had stayed hidden for the past three years. Rick didn't trust his guys to handle any shipments on their own. We would be able to put him away for good if we caught him in the act during this next shipment.

Daniel answered on the first ring. I filled him in on the news from Dino.

"You think we need another guy to go under?" he asked.

"I don't think it'd be a bad idea. Evan is always ready to go into the field."

"Prep him and send him out Friday night."

"Yes, sir."

Evan was happy to hear he would finally be getting more than desk work for a few months. I was glad to be gaining some momentum on the case, but I knew I'd be too busy to see Payton for at least two weeks. I'd spend this week prepping Evan and the next week being his shadow to make sure the group took him in.

Payton

"Tomorrow is the day, huh?" Gretta asked as she sipped her morning coffee.

"Yeah, my appointment is at 8am. I'm sort of nervous."

"Well, I'd go with ya if I didn't have to be here. Everything will be fine, dear. Don't waste your time worrying."

I promised her I would try not to worry as I laid the money for my breakfast on the table.

"Enjoy your day off!" Gretta called as I walked out the door.

I was starting to hate my days off. I didn't spend them relaxing or cleaning or shopping. I spent them thinking about L.A. and how my life would have been if I'd never met Sean. If I would have moved away for college and started my own life instead of staying close to home and close to my family. I knew what they were doing, I knew who my father was, and still, I stayed. I didn't help make the cocaine or other drugs, and I didn't help sell it. There had been a few times that my father had sent me to collect money from his dealers. I should have said no. I should have put distance between us. Instead, I stuck around and was there the night my parents died. The officers in L.A. didn't know who had killed them. But I knew. I knew it was my father's own guys. They'd finally gotten sick of doing all the work and him getting all the profit. He'd put hits out on one too many people, and they made him pay for it. Not only him, but my mother, brother, and Sean paid for it, too. They had to get rid of the few loyal people who were left.

I rubbed my stomach while the baby tossed and turned. My baby would never have grandparents or even a father. Sean would have been a shitty dad, that's a given, but now my child would never have the chance to know him. Mom would have been a fantastic grandma, or "Nana." She had told me that she wanted to be called "Nana" by all of my children. I didn't bother telling her I wouldn't be having more than one; I didn't want to kill her happy moment. I know dad would have loved my child as much as he loved me, but a part of me felt relieved that my child wouldn't be brought up the way that I was.

I was just waking up from a nap when the doorbell rang. I'd fallen asleep on the couch watching a movie. I stretched my arms and roughly ran my fingers through my hair before opening the door. When I saw who it was, I immediately regretted not looking in the mirror first.

"I went to the restaurant first. They said you were off the next couple of days. Is it okay that I came by?" Gavin asked. How am I supposed to say no to the guy? I mean, he did spend an entire day shopping with me. Not to mention how adorable he looked standing on my porch with his hands tucked in his pockets.

"Come on in," I said as I kicked the door further open.

"Looks like you're having a nice day off," he said, looking at the pillow and blanket on the couch.

"It hasn't been too exciting, honestly."

"Well, let's do something exciting."

"Like?" I asked with a raised eyebrow.

"Anything you want, Payton."

"I hate to break it to you, but pregnant girls aren't all that exciting," I said, laying a hand on my stomach.

"Is that so? And how is the whole pregnancy thing going?"

"It's good. I mean, the peeing thirty times a day and the aching feet are getting a little old, but that's just part of it."

"I guess you're right," he laughed. "So is it a boy or a girl?"

"I'm not sure. I actually get to find out tomorrow. Well, as long as the baby cooperates."

Gavin's eyes doubled in size. "You get to find out tomorrow? You get to see the baby?"

I nodded as I tried to hide how nervous I was about the appointment.

Gavin

I sat on her couch and pretended to watch whatever was playing on her TV. She gets to see the baby tomorrow. She gets to know if it's a boy or a girl. I had no idea that happened this soon. I wanted to be there for that. I hadn't had enough time with her, though. I couldn't just barge in on one of her most important appointments. I didn't even know if she considered us friends.

"So, what are the names?" I asked without looking at her.

"What names? The baby's name?"

"Yeah, don't you have a boy name and a girl name picked out already?"

Her face turned red as she slowly shook her head. "It's too hard to choose. The kid is going to be stuck with the name I pick for their whole life. What if it's terrible?"

I probably shouldn't have laughed. Judging by the scowl on her face, I knew I shouldn't have laughed. But the way her eyes got wide just thinking about choosing a name for her child was adorable. Out of all the things she had to be scared of, she chose this.

"Well, that's what you're doing today. You're choosing a boy name and a girl name. You're also going to get a cell phone so I can call you and find out what ya got in there," I said with a wink. She blushed again and I couldn't take my eyes off of her.

"Let's do the cell phone first," she said. "Let me change, then we can go into Birmingham." She walked down the hall to her bedroom and came back in under ten minutes. She had the same yoga pants on and a light pink top. Her stomach was still so small that it was hard to believe that there was an actual baby inside it. She was pulling her hair up on top of her head as she walked to the front door.

"If you want to drive separately I can just follow you. There's no point in you coming back here just to have to turn around again."

"Uh, well, I usually stay in a hotel when I come here," I said quietly.

She raised an eyebrow and stared at me for a few seconds. "Why would you stay in a hotel? It's not that far of a drive."

"I just like to stick around for a couple days. On the off chance that you want to hang out with me." I smiled at her trying to lighten the mood.

"You're serious?"

I nodded.

"Well, you're not staying in a hotel tonight. You can stay here. The couch can't be any worse than a hotel bed."

I tried not to look as shocked as I felt. I opened the front door and started walking to my truck.

"Let's go before you change your mind," I called.

She laughed as she shook her head at me.

I spent the trip pretending I wasn't excited to be staying at her place. People didn't let strangers stay in their house. We were friends and she trusted me, at least a little.

We were on our way back to Payton's when I brought up the names again.

"I kind of like the name Karsen. I think if I have a boy, I'll end up naming him that."

"I like it. I'm sure he would like it, too," I joked.

"I don't have any girl names picked out. I want to have a girl the most. Is that bad?"

"Why do you want a girl the most?"

"I'm afraid of raising a boy by myself," she whispered.

I glanced over at her. I could see the worried expression on her face as she stared out her window.

"Hey," I waited for her to look at me before finishing what I was going to say. "You're going to be fine. You will be a great mom. That little boy or girl will be lucky to have you."

She nodded and wiped a tear from cheek. We were quiet until we pulled into her driveway. I grabbed the bag of stuff she'd gotten from the cellular store and the bag of clothes I'd brought with me. She was standing in the kitchen with her hands on her hips when I walked in. I raised an eyebrow at her.

"This thing that we're doing is weird. You want me to get to know you. For what? So you can keep a closer eye on me? So we can be friends? So we can be more than friends? What are we doing here?"

I sat everything down on the couch before walking over to her. I stopped with just a few inches separating her stomach from mine.

"So we can be more," I answered her honestly.

She blinked a couple times before looking up at me. After a moment she raised her eyebrows and said, "Okay."

"Okay?" I asked her.

She nodded and walked away toward her room. I heard her bedroom door click shut seconds later. I shook my head as I held in my laugh. This girl was something else.

***

The sun shining through a window woke me up the next morning. I grabbed my phone and saw that it was after 7am. I hopped off the couch and looked in the driveway. Payton's Jeep was still outside. I walked down the hall and quietly knocked on her door.

"Payton? Are you awake?" When she didn't answer I slowly opened the door. She was curled up on her side, laying on top of her blankets. She was dressed in a new set of clothes so I knew she was awake. I sat down beside her and leaned over to see her face. She looked back at me with red rimmed eyes.

"What are you doing?" I whispered.

"Being ridiculous," she whispered back.

I smiled at her. "What's wrong?"

"I'm scared. What if something is wrong? They'll see it today, then I'll spend the next four months freaking out about it. What if it's something really terrible?" Her bottom lip quivered and my heart hurt for her. I moved the hair out of her face and left my hand resting on her cheek. She closed her eyes and took a shaky breath.

"I think I'm going to reschedule my appointment," she said quietly.

"Payton, it's okay that you're scared. Hell, it's probably normal for you to be scared. But you and I both know you will still be scared next week, or even next month. Rescheduling will only give you more time to worry about it.

You're dressed and ready to go. You can do this."

She sniffed a couple times before sitting up. "You're right. I've got to go today."

I nodded at her and stood up and grabbed her hand to help her off the bed. She glanced at our hands together, then up at me. Her eyes took their time making their way up to my face, but I didn't mind. I'd meant to put my shirt back on but forgot when I thought Payton was going to be late.

I winked at her when she finally looked at me and the blush on her cheeks made me laugh. She shook her head and stood up.

"You might want to put a shirt on before we leave," she said as she walked out of her room.

"Before *we* leave?" I asked, following her.

"I just told you that I'm terrified. You're really going to make me go alone?"

She was letting me go? Not just *letting*, but *telling* me to? I was going to get to see the baby? I sprang into action, slipping a clean shirt over my head as I jogged to the bathroom to brush my teeth. We were out the door in three minutes tops.

Payton drove and I sat in the passenger seat, smiling like an idiot. We parked and made our way toward the front door of the doctor's office. Payton stopped walking, and when I looked back at her I could tell that her face was pale. I grabbed her hand and realized it was shaking a little. Without thinking, I wrapped my arms around her and pulled her in tight to my chest.

"Everything will be fine," I told her.

She hugged me back and nodded. She took a deep breath, and I let her go. She grabbed my hand and laced her fingers with mine before walking inside.

The nurse was ready to take her back as soon as we walked in. I tried to let go of her hand in case she wanted me to wait in the waiting room. She squeezed my hand tighter, not letting me go. I was on cloud nine before we even made it to the exam room.

"Dr. Grey will be in shortly," the nurse told us.

"Thank you for coming with me, Gavin. I would have cancelled if you didn't."

"I'm happy to be here with you," I said honestly.

The doctor came in after tapping on the door. The same nurse came in behind her.

"Who do we have here?" the doctor asked as she looked me up and down.

"Gavin Sparks. I'm a friend of Payton's," I said, shaking her hand.

"Pleased to meet you. I'm Dr. Grey." I nodded and sat back down.

"So, how are you feeling, Payton?"

"I'm tired a lot. But I feel fine other than that."

"That's pretty normal. Were you wanting to know the sex of the baby today?"

Payton glanced at me before nodding to the doctor.

"Great. Go ahead and lift your shirt up and lay back for me."

I watched as Payton did as she was told. My breath hitched as I looked at her bare stomach. She was beautiful.

"Gavin, you can come stand beside the table if you'd like a closer look," the nurse said. I looked at Payton and she nodded her agreement. I took a deep breath and made my way over to her.

"This will be a little cold at first, remember," Dr. Grey told Payton.

I grabbed Payton's hand and held it tight. I watched Dr. Grey put clear gel on her stomach and then my eyes were locked on the screen in front of us.

After a little maneuvering, a tiny hand and five little fingers came into focus. I heard Payton gasp, but I couldn't look away to see her reaction. Dr. Grey showed us the feet and toes next. I glanced at Payton and saw the tears welling up in her eyes. We saw several other body parts and Dr. Grey told us what was what. It all looked the same to me, but it was still amazing.

"Now, let's see the good stuff," she said with a wink.

I was torn between wanting to watch Payton and the screen. I decided to give Payton a little privacy and keep my focus on the screen.

"Do you see that, Payton?" the doctor asked her.

"See what?"

"I don't see anything, either," I said.

"Exactly, there's nothing down there."

Dr. Grey was smiling and I felt Payton let go of my hand to cover her mouth. I looked at the screen again and then looked at Payton. She was laughing and crying.

"What is it?" I asked, confused.

"It's a girl, Gavin," Dr. Grey said.

"A girl?" I asked with wide eyes. "You've got a little girl in there?"

Payton nodded. She was smiling the biggest I'd ever seen her smile.

Dr. Grey shook our hands and told the nurse to clean off Payton's belly. She told Payton to schedule another appointment for next month, and then she was gone. The nurse walked out seconds later.

I was still staring at Payton's stomach while she sat up. She tried to pull her shirt down, but I stopped her. I looked at her for permission as I reached out to touch her stomach. She nodded and leaned back onto her elbows. I swallowed hard and gently put my hand on her. I felt a small wave of movement under it and pulled my hand away quickly.

"That's her way of saying 'hello,'" Payton said, giggling.

I leaned down and put my mouth closer to her bare stomach, "Hello, little girl," I whispered. I felt the movement under my hand again and smiled. I pulled Payton's shirt down and gave her my hand to help her sit up again. She hopped off the table and threw her arms around me.

"She's perfect," she whispered against my neck.

I couldn't remember a time in my life when I'd been happier, and I wanted to show Payton that. I leaned back and gently pressed my lips to hers. I moved my mouth against hers slowly as I tried to tell her how happy I was for her through my kiss. When I pulled away, I kissed her forehead gently before grabbing her hand and walking her out to my truck.

Payton

I waved to Gretta as I sat down at my usual table. It had been a week since I'd told her I was having a little girl, but she still smiled bigger than usual and patted my stomach every chance she got.

"I'll take the usual," I told her as she sat down across from me.

"Kitchen is already workin' on it. How are my girls doin'?"

"We're doing just fine. Exhausted, but fine," I said as I rubbed my belly.

"Mhm, and what about Gavin? How is he?" she asked with raised brows.

I had told Gretta about Gavin kissing me after my appointment last week. She had scolded me for not pursuing anything with him. According to her, it was obvious we had a *"connection."*

"I assume he's fine as well. I haven't seen him in a week."

"Well, that ain't for his lack of tryin' I'm sure. You want to go through your new life alone, so be it. But don't you come cryin' to me about being lonely when you have a perfectly good man waiting to sweep you off your feet," she huffed, shaking her head.

"Gretta, just because he stops in to eat breakfast with you occasionally does not mean he is a perfectly good man. And, just because he wants to be here for me now doesn't mean it's going to last. As soon as things get tough, he'll bail. Just like Sean."

As far as Gretta knew, the father of my child was Sean Cooper from Oklahoma, and he'd left me as soon as he had found out I was pregnant.

Gretta had a sad look on her face as she slowly shook her head. "All I'm saying is to be his friend. You can't keep spending all your free time with the likes of me. Stop ignoring him and just roll with the punches."

A man from the kitchen brought me my breakfast and interrupted the lecture I was getting. We talked about little things like the weather and the upcoming time change while I ate.

I got to work just as Hannah was flipping the closed sign around to say open. She waved as I got out of my Jeep and made my way inside.

"Hey, how was your night off?"

"Uneventful," I shrugged.

"Wow, sounds like my night at work," she joked.

"In that case, you can have the first table today. I'm tired anyways."

"Deal. You know, you don't have to work so many doubles. We can all see that you're worn out by the end of the night. Why don't you tell mom and dad you just want lunch shifts?"

"I can handle it for a few more months," I assured her. The truth was, I hated being home alone all the time. I'd rather be working.

It was almost closing time when a group of guys came in. I watched the four of them as Hannah seated them in my section. Twenty minutes until closing time and they decide to come in. I ground my teeth in frustration before going to take their drink orders.

"Hi, I'm Payton and I'll be your server tonight," I said in a sweet tone. "What can I get you all?"

"You all, huh? You ain't from around here are ya?" the bozo to my left asked.

"Oklahoma," I said as I shook my head at him.

"I thought Okies said y'all, too," another guy said with a confused look on his face.

"Guys, leave the lady alone and order your food. She's obviously ready to get home and put her feet up." I looked down at the guy to my right. He was wearing a baseball hat and an Alabama football shirt. He was smiling at me and I smiled back, silently thanking him for keeping his friends in line.

Luckily, they ordered their drinks and their meal at the same time. Maybe I wouldn't have to work as late as I'd thought.

"You know, you look familiar," the guy in the hat said.

I forced myself not to roll my eyes at his lame attempt at a pick-up line. "We haven't met," I said shortly. "Is there anything else you need?"

"What's your name again?" baseball hat guy asked.

"It's Payton."

"I'm Chad. Chad Granger. It's nice to meet you," he said with a wink.

I shook his outstretched hand and smiled at him. He was a looker, that's for sure. If I weren't so tired I would have been more eager to chit-chat, but my back was killing me and images of my bed kept flitting through my head.

"Go home. I've got your last table," Hannah said from behind me.

"I'm fine; they'll be finished soon. You can head out. I can handle the cleaning."

"You sure?"

I nodded. She hugged me tight, like I'd done her some huge favor by letting her leave thirty minutes early.

"See you in the mornin'," she called over her shoulder as she skipped out the back door.

I folded silverware at a table toward the back of the restaurant until it looked like the guys at my table were finished. I started walking over to deliver their ticket and Chad handed me a one hundred dollar bill.

"Keep the change."

"Uh, are you sure? The bill was only for forty-eight dollars," I told him.

"Positive," he winked.

"Well, thanks. You guys have a good night."

They all stood and I started piling plates on top of each other. I felt a hand on my lower back and jerked around. It was Chad. His eyes were intense and they were going over every part of my face.

"Are you sure your name's Payton? Because you look a lot like a girl I knew when I was a kid," he said without moving away from me.

I took a step to the side to give myself some space. My stomach was churning. I didn't recognize this guy; it had to be some sort of weird coincidence. Right?

"I guess I just have one of those faces," I shrugged, trying to play it cool.

"I guess you're right. See you around, Payton."

I watched him as he walked out of the restaurant. I let out the breath I'd been holding as soon as the door closed. I cleaned as quickly as possible and headed out the door. Once I was showered and in bed I sent a quick text to Gavin. *How are things?*

He replied instantly. *Tired of ignoring me now?*

I rolled my eyes at his message. Okay, I'd spent the last week ignoring his messages. Not without good reason, though. *That depends, are you going to kiss me again?*

Definitely not…Until you ask me to kiss you…

I couldn't help but smile. *Then I won't be ignoring you. Until you ask me to ignore you.*

I'd never ask you to do that. Where are you?

Just got in from work.

Less than a minute after I'd hit send, my doorbell rang. I jumped at the sound. Then, I started smiling as I went to the front door. I had expected to see Gavin on my porch, but he wasn't there. Instead, there were a dozen roses lying on my welcome mat. I looked out into the darkness, and when I didn't see anything or anyone, I picked them up and went inside. There was a handwritten note attached to the bundle of roses that read,

Can't wait to see you again

-CG

Who the heck was CG? And if they can't wait to see me then why did they ring my doorbell and leave? At least if they would have waited they would have seen that they had the wrong house because I didn't know anybody who would be sending me flowers.

I called Gavin, you know, to make sure he didn't send me flowers and sign the wrong initials. I'm sure that happens more often than not.

"Sparks," he said in way of greeting.

"Did you send me roses?" I asked, trying to get straight to the point.

"No. Was I supposed to send you roses?"

"No."

"Wouldn't that make you ignore me for another week?" he asked.

"It's a possibility, but somebody definitely sent me roses. There's a note, too."

"Did a delivery guy bring them to your work or to your house?" he asked. His voice wasn't as playful now.

"There was no delivery guy. Someone rang my doorbell five minutes ago and when I opened the door nobody was there. The roses were just lying on the ground," I explained.

"Five minutes ago? It's almost eleven o'clock at night! Why would you answer the door this late?" I could tell he was getting angry.

"I thought it was you," I mumbled into the phone.

His voice was calmer now that he'd heard my explanation, but I could still hear a hint of panic. "What? No, it wasn't me. I'm on my way now though. Leave the door locked until I get there."

I heard the slam of his truck door before the call ended.

Gavin

Thank God I had decided to stay in the hotel again tonight. Payton hadn't returned any of my calls or messages in eight days. I was prepared to go to her place first thing in the morning to set things straight. I had been surprised to see her name show up on my screen when she'd texted me. I was even more surprised when she called me. I wished I was going to her place just to see her, but something wasn't right. Somebody she didn't know knew where she lived and had already been at her house once. I was going over there to find out who it was and what they wanted with Payton.

She opened her door before I had a chance to knock.

"Hey," I said awkwardly

"What's going on? Why are you freaking out about the flowers? Isn't it normal for people to get flowers?"

"Sometimes, yes. Do you have anybody around here that would feel like sending you flowers? And even if you did, does anybody but me know your address?"

I took her silence as a no and continued. "That's why I'm here. I want to see the note and see if we can figure out who dropped them off. I'm not freaking out; I don't freak out."

"Sure you don't," she laughed, handing me the note.

"Who's CG?" I asked her.

"I thought that's why you were here, to figure that out," she said, rolling her eyes.

"Well, do you know anybody with those initials?" I pressed.

"You and Gretta are the only people I know outside of work," she huffed.

"Okay, what about customers at work? Have any of them been overly friendly? Have you told any of them your full name?"

She looked up at the ceiling as she thought about what I'd asked her. She was running her fingers through the ends of her dark hair and I could tell she was chewing on the inside of her bottom lip.

"There were some guys tonight. Four of them. They were teasing me about the way I talk. They said they could tell I wasn't from around here. Then one of them said he thought I looked familiar. I assumed he was trying to pick me up because I was sure I'd never seen him before. But then he said it again before they left."

"Do you remember any of their names?"

"Only one of them told me his name. Shook my hand and everything," her eyes grew wide for a second.

"What? What was his name?" I asked impatiently.

"Chad. Chad Granger. That has to be who CG is!" she said smiling like a little girl who was proud of herself for completing a puzzle.

Now I was certain my eyes were the size of saucers. *Chad Granger??? Why the fuck would she be smiling about roses from one of the country's biggest drug lord's son?*

"Chad Granger? You're sure that's his name?" *Please let her be wrong. Please let it be a mistake. Don't let Granger have his sights set on her.*

"Yeah that's it. I'm positive. They could have followed me home from work. They left about ten minutes before I did."

I got a sick feeling in my stomach. Not only did Chad want her. Now, he knew where she lived.

"Pack a bag. You're staying with me for a few days," I demanded.

"What? No, I'm not. I've got to work the rest of this week," she argued with her hands on her hips.

I clenched my teeth and stalked to her bedroom. I found a Nike backpack in the top of her closet and started shoving things into it. I grabbed several shirts and pants. I was ready to rummage through the dresser when she jerked the bag out of my hand.

"What do you think you're doing?!" she yelled.

"Protecting you. Now get your shit together because we're leaving."

Her face was bright red, and I knew she was furious, but I was too mad to explain anything right now.

"Payton, I'm begging you. Please get your things and get in the truck. I'll explain more on the way."

After staring me down for a minute she finally gave in and threw some more things into her bag.

"Let's go, kidnapper," she huffed.

If I weren't so pissed, I would have laughed. Payton was so clueless about who Chad Granger was, and she refused to believe me when I told her that he was dangerous. In fact, she spent the entire ride rolling her eyes, shaking her head, and not speaking to me.

"He's just some guy who thinks getting me roses will make me an easy lay," she said as I was parking outside of my apartment complex.

I slammed the truck in park and stared at her. "You think this is a fucking joke, Payton?"

My words came out harsher than they should have, and I knew I shouldn't have dropped the f-bomb. I rubbed my face roughly with both hands before looking up at her. She was shooting daggers at me with her beautiful brown eyes.

"Payton, I'm sorry. It's just.."

"Save it. I want to go inside," she said before slamming the truck door in my face.

I unlocked the door and carried the bag Payton had packed into my bedroom. She didn't follow me. She was still standing in the doorway watching me as I tossed a pillow onto the black leather couch.

"Don't be mad at me," I pleaded as I walked over to her.

"Stop freaking out about nothing," she countered.

"Chad Granger's father is one of the main guys over drug trafficking throughout the country. Chad works for him and he's had countless accusations brought against him. Everything from theft and assault to stalking and rape. I'm not freaking out. And if I were, I promise you it's not about nothing."

Her mouth dropped open and she took in a deep breath.

"I want you to stay here with me for the week. We will see if he makes any more advances and go from there. You'll need to call the restaurant and let them know you will be back Saturday." I was quiet for a moment, trying to gauge her reaction, but she said nothing.

She finally nodded and I released the breath I hadn't realized I had been holding. She might not be happy about it, but she had agreed to let me protect her.

"You can sleep in my room. I'll take the couch."

"Can I shower first?" she asked quietly.

I showed her to the bathroom before making myself comfortable on the couch. As comfortable as possible, anyway. I must have fallen asleep before she was finished in the bathroom.

I woke up and had to peel myself off of the leather couch so I could reach my phone. After seeing it was only 3am, I realized I was in for a long week. The couch was probably the most uncomfortable one I'd ever slept on. *You're keeping Payton safe,* I repeated to myself for the one hundredth time.

Payton

I'd been trying to convince myself to get up from my *Lifetime* movie marathon and take a shower when my phone buzzed with a text. It was Gavin. *How are you?*

Good. Just staring at the TV.

Want me to bring dinner?

Now I was interested. *Pizza?*

Perfect. See you at 6. I was shocked that he would be back at so early. I'd stayed with him for the past three nights, and he had yet to be home before 10pm. He was always gone before I woke up, too. We had barely seen each other since I'd been staying with him, and I was going out of my mind with boredom.

I had over an hour to wait on him, so I took my time in the shower. I secretly loved using his body wash. I had packed my own, but I couldn't resist using his. It smelled delicious, I swear.

After my extra-long shower, I towel dried my hair and ran my fingers through it. My Nike running shorts and loose t-shirt seemed like a good outfit to pair with my wet, wavy hair. I was in the middle of putting a second coat of black nail polish on my toes when Gavin walked in.

"Honey, I'm home," he teased. "And I brought pizza."

"It smells great. I'll be done in just a second."

He didn't say anything, and I didn't hear him walk away, so I looked up from my wet toes. He was staring right at me.

"What are you looking at?" I asked, raising an eyebrow at him.

"You. You look cute like that," he said with a smirk.

I rolled my eyes and focused back on my feet as I tried to hide the blush that was surely creeping up on my cheeks. I heard him chuckle as he walked away.

Once my toes were dry and I had a pile of pizza on my plate, I got comfortable on the couch while Gavin watched something on the *History* channel.

"How are you feeling today?" he asked before taking a drink of his water.

"I feel fine. It's really boring here, so I've caught up on my sleep."

"Well, that makes one of us," he said with a wink.

"What time do you actually have to be at work? You're always gone so early."

"I usually don't go in until eight, but I've been waking up early this week."

"The couch isn't doing it for you?" I asked with a grin.

"Not exactly," he laughed.

"Well, why don't you sleep in your bed? With me?"

He choked on his water and started coughing. Once he had his composure back he narrowed his eyes at me. "Stop messing with me," he said.

"Suit yourself," I mumbled around a piece of pizza.

I saw him look at me out of the corner of his eye a couple of times while we watched TV together. I knew he was trying to figure out if I was being serious about sharing a bed with him or not. I was. Why wouldn't I want to share a bed with a muscled up detective who was sporting a nice tan and a sleeve of tattoos?

When I couldn't stop yawning, I cleaned up the pizza trash and went to get ready for bed. When I opened the door to Gavin's bedroom, he was sitting on the edge of his bed.

"Is it really okay if I sleep in here? I mean, I'll stay on my side and I can use a separate blanket if you want." His left hand was squeezing the back of his neck as he nervously waited for my response.

"Gavin, get your ass in the bed and stop freaking out over nothing," I teased. He laughed before throwing a pillow at me. I chunked it back and crawled under the covers for protection.

His laugh was muffled by something, and I peeked out from under the blanket to see what it was. He was slipping his black t-shirt off. I was taking him all in, the ridges of his muscular back and arms. The black and grey tattoos that went from the middle of his back to his shoulder and down the length of his arm. I was too busy staring to realize he was undoing his jeans, too. They ended up in a messy pile right next to his shirt. *Game over*, I thought to myself.

"I've got to get some sleep tonight, so don't get any ideas," he joked as he climbed into the bed.

"Only in your dreams," I quipped.

"If you only knew," he muttered as he reached up to pull the chain hanging from the light. I was thankful for the darkness because I knew my cheeks were red hot.

We lay there, facing away from each other and awkwardly whispered "goodnight."

***

I was standing on my parent's roof, right outside of the tiny bathroom window. I was crying. Sean had just told me he wouldn't live through the night. I knew my brother and my parents were all going to die as well. I pressed my hand to my flat stomach and prepared myself to jump to the tree.

"She broke the window! I can't fit!" I heard a deep voice yell from inside of the house.

I glanced down the street to see the flashing lights that were getting closer by the second. Without giving myself a chance to change my mind, I took a deep breath and jumped. I slid down the side of the tree a bit before I was able to grab onto a limb and pull myself up to sit on it. My arms and legs were covered in scratches and I knew they would be hurting once the adrenaline wore off.

"Miss, are you okay?" a familiar voice called from below me.

I looked down to see an officer standing at the bottom of the tree. His arms were outstretched for me.

"You're going to be okay, Haley. I'm going to take care of you. Just take my hand," the officer told me.

I heard what he was saying, but I didn't believe him. The cops knew the things my family was into. I knew the second I came down he would throw some cuffs on me and take me downtown.

The gunshots that were fired inside of the house startled me and I lost my balance. The officer caught me before I fell to the ground. He hugged me to his chest as he whispered things that I'm sure were meant to be comforting. But I couldn't understand him because I was sobbing uncontrollably.

***

"Payton? Wake up. It's just a dream. I've got you."

Gavin's soothing whispers pulled me out of my nightmare. I had to blink a couple of times before my eyes adjusted to the darkness. Gavin was propped up on his elbow and facing me.

His other hand was resting on my cheek, and he had a worried expression on his face.

"You were crying," he said quietly.

His hand fell from my face as I sat up and wiped my tears on my t-shirt. After taking a few calming breaths, I let myself fall back onto the pillow.

"Just a bad dream, I guess," I shrugged. I didn't want to go into detail about it and I hoped he wouldn't ask.

To my relief, he fell back onto his pillow and grabbed my hand. He laced our fingers together and gently rubbed my palm with his thumb. He didn't say anything else, and neither did I. We just laid there in the dark until I finally dozed off again.

I woke up to an empty bed. I assumed Gavin had already left for work until I heard his voice down the hall.

"I'll stop by tomorrow before I leave town. Until then, you can reach me on my cell."

I could tell he was on the phone by the pauses in the conversation. After a brief silence of him listening to what the person on the other line had to say, he started talking again.

"She doesn't know, and I'm going to keep it that way for now. Understood?"

Another brief pause.

"See you tomorrow."

I heard his footsteps coming down the hall and rolled over like I was sleeping. The door barely squeaked when he opened it. I laid there, waiting for him to shut it and walk back down the hall, but he didn't. Instead, he lay down next to me on top of the blanket. I rolled over to face him. He was wearing black sweats and a white t-shirt, his tattoo-covered arm was resting behind his head.

"It's about time you woke up," he said.

"Shouldn't you be working?"

"I took the day off. I know you've been going out of your mind with boredom, so I thought we would go do something fun today."

"What's your definition of fun, Gavin?" I asked while narrowing my eyes at him.

"I thought we could go shopping for your baby. You need a crib, ya know. And I'm sure she would appreciate having some clothes when she gets here," he teased.

"Really? You want to go baby shopping with me?" I asked as I sat up.

"If you want me to go," he shrugged.

"Yes! I'll go get ready!"

Gavin

After six long hours of shopping, we had scheduled a delivery truck to drop off a crib and changing table at Payton's house tomorrow evening. Payton had found wall decorations for the nursery and had picked out at least a closet full of outfits. A weaker man might have been embarrassed to admit that he knew over a hundred different shades of pink. However, I'd do the same thing again tomorrow if it made her as happy as she was when we left the baby store that day.

We had just walked into my apartment when Payton collapsed onto the couch.

"Will you take my shoes off?" she mumbled.

I shook my head and chuckled before slipping off her brown sandals. Once the shoes were out of the way, I sat down and put her feet in my lap and started massaging them.

She let out an exaggerated moan and closed her eyes.

"You've been holding out on me," she smirked.

"Don't get used to it. Foot rubs are reserved for special occasions only."

"Why are you so nice to me?" she asked quietly.

"Just a few days ago you were pissed at me for kidnapping you. One foot rub and I'm back in your good graces? That was easy enough," I joked.

She used the foot I wasn't rubbing to kick me in the thigh. "I'm serious," she huffed. "You barely know me, but you go out of your way to make sure I'm happy. Why?"

I studied her as I considered her question. I couldn't tell her the truth. I couldn't tell her that I did know her, that I'd known her and her family for years. I stared at her feet in my lap as I told her a half truth, unable to make eye contact with her.

"It doesn't count as going out of my way when seeing you happy makes me happy, too. I've seen your mad face plenty of times, and last night during your dream I saw your sad face.

You're not meant to be mad or sad, Payton. Your happy face is the only one I want to see when I'm with you."

She sat up and tucked her feet under her so she was sitting on her knees. She leaned in and pecked my cheek. I breathed in, shocked by her closeness. "I like your happy face, too, Gavin. But your mad face is kinda sexy, so it's my favorite."

And with that she was off the couch and walking down the hall. I blew out the breath I had sucked in and shook my head. This woman and her mind games were testing my sanity.

"Where are you going? We were just getting to the good part!" I called after her.

She didn't say anything, but I heard her giggle before the shower started running. I waited a beat, trying to think about what I was about to do. In the end, I gave up trying to think anything through. I jumped off the couch and stalked to the bathroom.

I opened the door and let it bang against the wall behind it so she'd know I was coming in. The mirror was already fogged over from steam, along with the glass door leading to the small walk in shower.

I could tell by her silhouette that her arms were crossed over her chest.

"Payton, we aren't done with this conversation. Start talking, or I'm opening the door."

A few seconds of silence passed between us. I pulled my shirt over my head and unbuttoned my jeans. "Have it your way," I told her.

"Wait! What do you want me to say, Gavin?"

"I want you to tell me the truth, about everything. Can you?"

"I'll try," she said so quietly I could barely hear her over the shower.

"Why did you ignore me after I kissed you?"

"Because I was mad at you. You don't kiss someone you don't know like that. A kiss like that is meant for someone you care about. Not for someone you feel sorry for."

"Feel sorry for? Why would I feel sorry for you, Payton?" I asked through gritted teeth. I could still see her shadow through the glass door and forced myself to turn away. I gripped the edge of the sink as I listened to her response. It took all my effort not to break it.

"Gee, I don't know, Gavin. Maybe because I'm six months pregnant with no family and no friends. Who wouldn't feel sorry for the pregnant girl who's completely alone?" Her voice broke at the end of her sentence and I knew she was crying.

I grabbed a towel out of the cabinet and held it out to her as I opened the glass door. "Get out," I ordered, keeping my eyes closed tight. She turned off the water and then took the towel from me. I felt her brush past me and I opened my eyes just in time to see her slam my bedroom door.

I gritted my teeth to keep from yelling and opened the door. Payton was sitting on the edge of the bed wiping the tears from her eyes with the towel she was wrapped in.

I knelt down in front of her and waited for her to look at me. "I'm done talking about this, Gavin."

"I'm not finished yet, Payton. I have never felt sorry for you. And I sure as hell wouldn't kiss you out of pity. I care about you, Payton."

She turned her head away from me and gently shook her head.

"Look at me," I ordered. "I do care about you, and I care about her," I said as I put my hands on either side of her belly.

"Let me, Payton. Let me care about both of you," I pleaded.

I felt a thud against my left hand and looked down at Payton's belly. I felt it again in the same spot and her hand covered mine, pressing it down harder. I could feel her tossing and turning under the towel.

"I guess she likes you, too," Payton whispered with tear-stained cheeks.

"Now we have to convince your mom that I'm worth keeping around," I whispered to her stomach. I looked up and saw Payton smiling down at me. The knot that was in my stomach started to ease, and I took in a calming breath before getting to my feet.

Payton stood when I did. I was turning to walk out and give her some privacy when she threw her arms around my neck. I was still for half a second, due to shock. Then, I wrapped my arms around her waist and hugged her tight. I could have held her for hours if she were wearing more than a towel. But I knew my resolve wouldn't last long, so I let her go and let her get dressed.

Payton

"My table is requesting you. It's some guy. I sat him in the booth at the back," Hannah said as she was pouring a customer's drink into a to-go cup.

"Oh, okay. Go ahead and cut me off after this one, my feet are killing me," I groaned.

I was surprised to see Chad Granger sitting at the booth. A part of me had hoped it would be Gavin, but I knew he would be busy at work until the weekend. I paused for a second, considering making Hannah take care of him. When I considered the fact that she had three other tables and had to come back and close tonight, I took a deep breath, put on a fake smile, and walked over to his table.

"Can I get you something to drink, sir?" I asked. I looked through him like I didn't recognize him. He smirked up at me.

"Long time, no see, Payton. Did you have a nice vacation?"

"Uh, sorry, have we met?" I asked, feigning confusion.

"Just once, about two weeks ago. I came in right before closing time with a few friends. Chad Granger," he said offering me his hand.

"Oh! Now I remember. Good to see you again. What can I get you to drink, Chad?"

He just stared at me with a grin on his face. I nervously tucked my hair behind my ear and started listing our drink options.

"Coke, Diet Coke, Sprite, tea, coffee?"

He chuckled as he nodded his head. "Honestly, I didn't come here to eat. Or to get a drink. I just wanted to see you," he said as he looked up at me from under his baseball cap.

I got a nervous feeling in my stomach. I planned on calling Gavin as soon as I got off work.

"Why would you want to see me?" I asked him.

"Aside from the fact that you're gorgeous, there is no reason. You look like you would make a pretty good friend and I'm always looking to lengthen my list of good friends," he said with a wink.

I had to force myself not to gag in front of him. *Who does this guy think he is?*

"Well, unfortunately, I prefer to keep my friends list very short. But I'll keep you in mind," I told him with a sweet smile.

He narrowed his eyes on me and I could tell he was angry. I refused to let myself be intimidated by this douchebag, so I stood my ground and held his stare.

He shook his head as he slid out of the booth. "Ya know, I thought you were smarter than that, Payton. I'll be seeing ya; count on that."

I didn't say anything as I watched him walk out the door. I cleaned the table he had sat at while Craig cashed me out. I wasted a few more minutes talking to Hannah before walking out the back door. I opened the door slowly and looked around to make sure Chad hadn't decided to wait around on me.

When I was certain nobody was around, I walked as fast as my aching feet could go toward the Jeep. It had been a week since I'd seen Gavin, but we'd talked daily on the phone and through texts. I didn't hesitate to call him.

"I was just thinking about you," he said as a way of greeting.

The sound of his voice alone made me feel calmer. "Hey, are you too busy to talk?"

"Never. What's up?"

"Well," I started to tell him about Chad showing up at the restaurant and about me pissing him off, but I knew he would jump in his truck and haul ass to my place even though he was so busy at work. I couldn't be the reason he kept getting behind.

"I don't have to work tomorrow, and I was thinking we could get dinner tonight and I could stay with you. If you don't have any plans," I said nervously.

"You miss me already?" he teased.

"Shut up, Gavin. Are you busy or not?"

"Not. I can come to you if you want. I don't really want you to have to make the drive alone."

I smiled at his unnecessary worry. I grew up in L.A.; driving in Alabama was a breeze.

"It's nothing I can't handle," I assured him. "I'll meet you at your place around six, okay?"

"Alright. Text me when you leave your place and I'll finish things up here."

"Will do."

"Payton?"

"Yeah?"

"I know you like me," I could hear him chuckle before the line went dead.

"Jerk," I said to myself as I rolled my eyes and pulled into my garage. After making sure the door shut all the way, I went inside to take a quick shower.

I slipped into a pair of dark skinnies and pulled a light blue t-shirt over my damp hair. I knew it would be frizzy once it dried, so I put an extra ponytail holder on my wrist. I had just slipped my Converse on and was throwing my bathroom things into a bag when I heard a knock on my front door.

I looked through the peep hole but didn't see anyone. I swallowed the lump in my throat and put my hand over my belly as I opened the door. I scanned my yard and driveway looking for a person or vehicle, but there was nobody around. I caught sight of the roses on the ground just as I was going close the door. There was no card this time, but I knew exactly who they were from.

Leaving the roses on the porch, I locked the door, grabbed my bag, and ran to the garage. I sent Gavin a text letting him know I was on my way while I waited for the door to rise. I knocked on his door less than an hour later.

"Well, you were obviously speeding," he said as the door swung open. After noticing the worried look on my face, his smile fell and he drew his eyebrows together. "Payton, what's wrong?"

I took a deep breath and walked inside to set my bag on his couch. "Chad Granger was at the steakhouse again tonight," I mumbled with my back to him. When he didn't say anything I thought he hadn't heard me, but then I turned to face him. The look on his face wasn't angry like I had expected. No, he wasn't angry at all, he was scared, and that terrified me even more.

Putting on a poker face, he asked, "Did he talk to you?"

I nodded. "He requested me as his waitress."

"What did he want?" Gavin ground out.

"Well, I acted like I didn't recognize him at first. Then, he told me I was gorgeous and that we would make good friends. I shot his idea down and he got mad. He said I could count on seeing him again. I waited a while to leave just in case he was waiting on me."

"Why didn't you call me, Payton?" he asked. Sounding even more pissed off.

"I did, as soon as I left work. I knew you would make me come stay with you again, so that's what I'm doing."

"You should have told me as soon as you called! You shouldn't have gone back to your house! What if he had been there waiting on you?" His face paled as he said it as if just the thought of that scenario made him sick.

"Well, when I got out of the shower I heard someone knock on my door. There were more roses on the porch. There wasn't a card this time, though. I left as soon as I saw them."

"Shit!" Gavin yelled while roughly running his fingers through his hair. "You're not going back to that restaurant or to your house until I get Chad Granger taken care of," he whispered harshly. I didn't have a chance to argue because he was stalking to his bedroom with his cellphone to his ear.

I fell onto the couch and brought my knees to my chest, well, as far as my belly would allow. I sat there, blinking back tears, trying to understand why this was happening to me.

Gavin

I had unintentionally spent over an hour on the phone with Evan. I was trying to gather all the information I could on Chad. Unfortunately, if we arrested him prematurely, we risked blowing our cover and tipping his father off. I would have to keep Payton with me until the upcoming shipment. Then, we could get Chad and his dad and put them away for good. Would she stay with me until then, though?

It didn't matter. I wasn't giving her a choice.

My anger dissipated when I saw her. She was laying on her side with her knees pulled to her. She had fallen asleep. She started to stir a little, so I scooped her up and carried her to the bedroom.

"What time is it?" she mumbled as I laid her down.

"It's three in the afternoon. Go ahead; take a nap."

She nodded as I pulled the blanket up over her. I closed the door as quietly as possible and headed downstairs to the gym.

I was glad to see that nobody else was in the gym when I got there. I needed time to think, and pushing my body to the limit was my favorite way to do it.

An hour later, I was soaked with sweat and breathing heavily. I felt better. More relaxed. I wished Payton would have called me the second Chad walked into that restaurant, but I was glad that she had at least made the right choice by coming to me. It was good that she was taking this more seriously than the last time. I shook my head and grinned as I remembered how pissed she was about staying with me a couple of weeks ago. Telling her that she was stuck here for at least two months this time should be fun, right?

When I walked back into my apartment it was still quiet and the bedroom door remained shut. I wanted to get in a quick shower before Payton woke up. I was peeling my sweat-soaked shirt over my head when I heard the door to my bedroom open.

She stood there, open-mouth staring at me. Her hair was a mess and her eyes were still puffy from sleeping. She was beautiful. She must have noticed that she was staring because her cheeks turned red and she quickly looked down at her feet. I held in my laugh as I walked toward her. "Nice nap?" I asked.

She nodded. "It would have been better if this little girl didn't kick me every time I got comfortable," she groaned as she playfully patted her belly.

"You've already got a little handful don't you?" I joked.

She smiled big as she looked up at me and nodded.

"I can't wait to meet her," I told her as I put both of my hands on her stomach.

She took in a shaky breath and looked away from me. "That's still another few months away, Gavin."

"I know; you're due in December. So?" I could feel the movement inside of her as I rubbed my thumbs back and forth.

"So we don't know where we will be by then. We might not even be friends anymore," she said with a shrug.

"Again with the nonchalant shit, Payton?" I asked, taking a step back and shaking my head.

"I'm just saying, this isn't anything serious. Don't feel obligated to do anything for us." She wouldn't look at me while she spoke, and that pissed me off even more. I gritted my teeth and stormed off to the bathroom. I took the hottest shower I could stand and didn't get out until I was sure I wouldn't yell at her. God knows I wanted to. *This isn't anything serious? Damn right it's not, because she won't let it be serious!*

I dried myself off and wrapped a black towel around my waist before walking across the hall to the bedroom. I didn't even look in the direction of where I heard the TV. I knew she was in there, though. My apartment felt ten times smaller when she was in it.

I put on my boxer-briefs and pulled my black sweats over them. I decided to forgo wearing a shirt for now. I didn't plan on leaving my room until I had thought of a plan. A plan to get Payton to see that I was serious about her, that I wanted her to be serious about me.

I sat on my bed and leaned against the headboard while I racked my brain. I was staring up at the ceiling when she knocked on the door.

"Yeah?" I asked without looking away from the ceiling.

"Can we talk?" she asked after clearing her throat.

"Come in," I sighed.

She opened the door slowly and shut it behind her. She'd never admit it, but I saw her eyes linger on my abs and chest before she met my eyes.

"I didn't mean to upset you earlier," she said quietly.

"I'm not upset. I'm fucking pissed, Payton. I thought we went over this two weeks ago. Why do you keep pushing me away when I finally get close?"

She drew her eyebrows together and frowned at me. "Well, I'm fucking pissed too, Gavin! Stop acting like you care so much when there is no way you do. Stop acting like you're in this for the long haul when I know you're not. Stop pretending to love my baby when you can't. If her own father couldn't, then how could you possibly care about her?" She had tears in her eyes and her voice broke on the last question. I stood up and rubbed my hands over my face as I tried to think of how to reply. How can I explain how much I do know her without telling her I met her when she was eighteen?

"Payton, I may not know everything about you. But, I do know that you're strong. You protected yourself from Tyler Donelli without a problem. I also know that you're brave. Brave enough to move away from everyone and everything you know and raise a child on your own. My favorite thing I know about you is the way you love. I see how much you love the little girl inside of you. I see it in your eyes every time you rest your hand on your stomach and every time you talk about her. I've never seen anyone care about someone as much as you care about her. How can anyone not care about her after seeing how much you care about her? Her father may not have been ready to be a part of her life, but I'm here, and I'm ready. I'm not pretending to care about either of you. This is real, Payton."

Tears were running down her cheeks. I took a step toward her, but she took two steps back and shook her head. "Don't push me away, Payton," I whispered as I wrapped my arms around her waist and pulled her to me.

"You don't have to stay, Gavin. Nobody stays," she mumbled into my chest. I squeezed her tighter as I gritted my teeth in attempt to hold in my anger. This beautiful girl had been let down her entire life, and she already had it in her mind that I would be letting her down, too.

"Hey," I said quietly and waited for her to look up at me. "I'm staying. Whether you want me or not, I'm not going anywhere." As soon as the words were out of my mouth, I kissed her. It took her a second to kiss me back, but it felt so good when she did. Our lips fell together perfectly, and I hated that it had been a month since I'd kissed her last. I'd never wait that long again.

After a minute she broke the kiss and tucked her head back into my chest as she hugged me tight. God, this girl, I would never get enough. I kissed her dark hair before releasing her and knelt down to kiss her stomach before I let her step back. She wiped her cheeks and smiled down at me. It was hard to tell if I'd gotten through to her or not, but I'd repeat myself as many times as she needed me to.

Payton

After almost an hour of arguing, I finally convinced Gavin to let me go to my doctor's appointment alone. He had planned on taking me, but there were a few things that had come up at work and he couldn't get away. I didn't want to have to reschedule on such short notice, and I was anxious to see how big my baby girl had gotten. Dr. Grey said she was growing right on schedule and that everything looked great. After my appointment next month, I would have to start going to see her every two weeks. I hoped I was back at my own place by then so I wouldn't have to drive as far.

I didn't tell Gavin I was planning on stopping by the restaurant. I knew he would tell me not to, but I wanted to be able to quit the right way. I owed Craig and Lisa more than a phone call, and I wanted to be able to tell Hannah goodbye.

After speaking with Lisa and Craig and hugging Hannah several times, I got in the Jeep and headed back to Gavin's. We were supposed to be going to dinner tonight when he got home. He said there was some Mexican place he wanted me to try. Things had gotten more relaxed between us over the last week. The only time things felt awkward was at night, right before bed. Gavin had gone back to sleeping on the couch, but he would come give me a quick kiss every night. And I'm not exaggerating when I say *quick* kiss. I barely had a chance to feel his lips before they were gone.

I know he was trying to give me space while I got used to having him there and having him care about me and my daughter, but that didn't mean we had to keep it G-rated, did it?

When I made it back to the apartment, I had a solid two hours to get ready. I texted Gavin to ask if the restaurant was casual or not. *It's a pretty simple place. Don't get dolled up on my account babe, I've already seen what you look like in the mornings. ;)*

You're hilarious.

See you in a couple of hours! I could just imagine the smirk on his face with that reply.

I rolled my eyes at my phone before tossing it on the bed and heading to the bathroom to get ready. I changed into a pair of jean shorts that looked like they were cut-offs but I'd actually bought them that way and a grey v-neck. I was curling my hair when I heard Gavin unlocking the door. I quickly sprayed hairspray all over my head and walked out to greet him.

I stopped at the end of the hallway when I realized he was on the phone.

"No, I didn't know she was going to the steakhouse. Thanks for letting me know. I'll handle it."

Shit. Who was he talking to?

"Thanks, Evan. I'll check in tomorrow. Same time."

He sat down on the couch and put his head in his hands. "Come here, Payton," he said without looking up.

I walked up behind the couch and wrapped my arms around his shoulders as I rested my head on his back. "Don't be mad at me," I pleaded.

He let out a heavy sigh and shook his head. I moved to sit down beside him but he hooked his arm around my waist and pulled me onto his lap.

"I'm not mad. But don't do it again."

"I wanted to quit my job the right way, Gavin. And I wanted to say goodbye to Hannah. How did Evan know I stopped by there?" I questioned.

"Evan is one of my undercover guys, Payton. He's been trailing Chad since the last time he sent you roses. He saw your Jeep there when he drove by. I can't protect you if I don't know where you are. Please just tell me where you are going next time."

I nodded and gave him a peck on his cheek, trying to lighten his mood. "I missed you today," he mumbled as he put his face in the crook of my neck. I involuntarily shivered when his warm breath blew over my skin.

"I'm sorry I didn't tell you about the restaurant. I promise I will next time" I felt guilty for worrying him so much. I gently rubbed his back as I waited for him to turn back into the playful Gavin I was used to.

"Are you hungry?" he mumbled against my neck.

I squirmed in his lap because it tickled. "I'm starving," I answered. I froze when I felt his tongue slide over the soft skin of my neck. His lips followed suit. "So am I," he said in a husky voice, causing me to swallow hard. I tilted my head to the side, offering him more of my neck.

"I should go change so we can leave," he said, leaving small pecks on my neck after each word.

I wanted to argue. Tell him that he should keep doing what he was doing; dinner could wait. But before I had the chance, my stomach let out a growl that sounded like I hadn't eaten in days.

"That settles it," Gavin said with a laugh. I slid off of his lap and he kissed my forehead before going to the bedroom to change.

"Thanks a lot," I told my stomach through gritted teeth.

Gavin came out of his room dressed in a pair of dark jeans and a white v-neck. After taking a second to look him over, I met his eyes and he winked at me.

"We'd better go before you wither away," he joked. I rolled my eyes and laughed as we walked out of his apartment.

The Mexican restaurant was casual, in a good way. There were several people there, so we sat at the bar instead of waiting for a table. Gavin ordered a Corona for himself and a water for me. We talked as we ate our chips and salsa, and by the time my enchiladas were ready I was too full to eat. Gavin laughed at me for filling up on chips instead of my actual dinner. He ate his fajitas and told me stories about him and his friends in college. I told him about my degree in marketing. He thinks I graduated from The University of Oklahoma. Other than that, I didn't go into much detail about my past, and I was relieved that he didn't ask. I was starting to realize that lying to him was going to be harder than lying to the others.

"I never asked how your appointment went today," he said before finishing off his second beer.

"Oh, it was fine. Dr. Grey said everything looks great. I go back in a month."

"Can I take you?"

"Gavin, I won't make any unnecessary stops. You don't have to do that," I told him, shaking my head.

"That's not why I want to take you, Payton. I just, I don't know. I want to be involved." I'm sure I stared at him with wide eyes for a minute before he finished by saying, "If you'll let me, I mean." It could have been the lighting in the restaurant, but I swear he blushed as he waited on me to reply.

"Sure, you can come," I said with a smile. He gave me an even bigger smile before throwing some cash on the bar and walking me out of the restaurant.

"Are you tired?" he asked as he parked in his usual parking spot outside of his apartment building.

"No," I answered, confused. "Should I be?"

"Well, you've yawned about thirty times since we left the restaurant. So either you're tired or I'm boring you."

"I'm not bored," I exclaimed, smacking his arm. "I might be a little tired," I said honestly.

He held my hand as we walked to his door. "Why don't you go ahead and lay down?

We can have breakfast tomorrow before I leave for work," he said once we were inside.

"It's barely eight o'clock. I can stay up a little longer."

"Whatever you want," he smirked.

"I'll go change. You start a movie." I walked into the bedroom. "Nothing scary!" I called out to him. I heard him chuckle as I slipped into a pair of Nike running shorts. I stopped by the bathroom to relieve myself, hoping that I could make it through the whole movie without having to ask him to pause it.

"Get comfortable," he said as he patted the couch next to him.

I sat down beside him as he hit play on a movie I knew I wouldn't be awake long enough to finish. I was going to give it a valiant effort, though.

I have no idea how much time passed between me getting comfortable on the couch and me waking up as Gavin laid me down in his bed.

"Is the movie over?" I mumbled, pulling the blanket up over my shoulders.

"It is for you," he chuckled. He bent over and kissed my forehead before turning to walk out.

"Are you going to sleep?" I asked.

"Yeah, I'm pretty tired, too."

"Sleep in here, Gavin. You'll rest better." He looked at me and back at the door twice. I moved over and pulled the covers back so he could get in, and that did it.

"Okay, just let me turn the light off in there," he said as he walked out.

I sat up and ran my fingers through my messy hair and rubbed my fingers under my eyes trying to make sure my makeup wasn't smudged. I laid back down when I heard his footsteps coming down the hall.

He turned the lamp on his dresser on before shutting the door. "Uh, Payton?" he asked awkwardly. "Do I need to sleep in my clothes?"

"Do you usually sleep naked?" I asked, and I could feel my face getting hot.

"No. I mean, I sleep in my underwear. But I can wear shorts and a shirt if you want," he said with a shrug.

"Gavin, you only wore your underwear the other times we've shared a bed. What's the big deal?"

He let out a sigh as he pulled his shirt over his head. "Well, Payton, that was before you started drooling every time you see me with my shirt off."

My mouth fell open and I chunked a pillow at him. "I do not drool!"

"Just try to keep it on your own pillow. Okay?" he joked as he pulled his jeans off. I rolled over and pulled the covers over my head.

I felt him situate the pillow I had thrown at him first. Then the bed dipped down as he lay down behind me.

"Okay, I'm completely covered. You can turn over now," he joked.

"I should have left you on the couch," I huffed. He laughed and tugged on my hip until I rolled to my back.

"I'd much rather be in here," he whispered. He leaned in and kissed my nose, then my forehead.

"You're lucky you're cute," I sighed. I felt his body shake as he laughed silently.

"I knew it," he whispered before kissing my lips.

"Knew what?" I questioned, breaking the kiss.

"That you think I'm cute. That you like me. That you want me to kiss you."

He started planting light kisses on the side of my neck that was closest to him. I formed a pouty face with my lips because he was right. About all of the above. I squeezed my eyes shut as I decided if that was all I wanted from him.

"And is that all I want?" I asked as confidently as I could.

He pulled away from my neck and looked at me. I could barely see him through the darkness, but I could tell his eyebrows were raised. I licked my lips and attempted to be seductive as I grabbed his face and pulled him down to me. My kiss was a little rougher than planned, but he got the memo. I tugged at his hair as he slipped his tongue into my mouth and deepened the kiss.

"I'm going to go out on a whim here and say no, that's not all you want," he said, slamming his mouth back down to mine, not giving me a chance to reply.

He threw the blanket to the foot of the bed and moved so he could lie on top of me. He used his arms to hold himself up, not touching my stomach at all. But his bottom half fit perfectly, just where I wanted it to. I put my legs around him and held in a moan as he rocked against me.

"Don't hide from me, Payton. I want to know what you like," he said, grinding against me again. I let out a breath and gripped his biceps.

"I don't know what I like," I told him, honestly. "I've only ever been with Sean, and I can't say there was much to like about it," I whispered, embarrassed by my lack of experience. Gavin stopped what he was doing and sat up, resting on his calves. "Payton, we don't have to do anything. You know that, right?" I nodded and looked away from him, even more embarrassed. He moved back to his side of the bed and I tried to turn away from him before he saw the tears welling in my eyes, but he placed his hand on my stomach and held me in place.

"Hey," he whispered. "I want you. More than anything. But tonight, let's just take it slow."

He lifted my t-shirt and started making slow circles on my belly. The little girl inside of me kicked his hand a couple of times and I giggled. "I'll never get tired of feeling her move," he said, kissing my cheek. I turned toward him so he could kiss my lips and he started playing with elastic on my shorts. I spread my legs for him, letting him know that it was okay. He slid his tongue into my mouth at the same time he pushed his hand under my panties.

"We're going to find out what you like," he said, breathing heavily in my ear.

Gavin

"Sparks, you've been smilin' nonstop all week. What's her name again?" Evan asked as he walked into my office, interrupting my thoughts of Payton.

"Shut up, Evan. You know its Payton. What do you want?"

"Just bringing you the files you asked for, Boss."

He laid both of the files on my desk. *Haley Golds. Sean Sanford.* "Thanks, man. Do me a favor and don't mention this to any of the others, alright?"

"Sure thing, Gavin. Anything I can help you with?"

I shook my head. "You just keep an eye on Chad and make sure he doesn't go near Payton."

He nodded before exiting my office. I opened Sean's file first. Now that Payton had come to terms with her feelings for me, I wanted to find out as much as possible about the father of her baby. Sean Sanford might get the privilege of being that little girl's biological father, but I was going to be her dad. No question about it.

The first page of his file was a copy of his death certificate, followed by several pictures of his dead body. I'd seen so many dead bodies over the past few years, I didn't even flinch now. But my heart ached for Payton and her loss.

I had just finished going over Sean's file when Daniel called me into his office. "What can I do for you?" I asked as I walked through his open door.

He pointed to the chair across from him and waited for me to sit. "Gavin, I need you to go U.C.," he said quietly. My mouth hung open for a second.

"What? You need me to go undercover? For what?" I tried to keep my panic at bay until I got the details.

"For the Granger case. I need more guys under. Guys with experience. Guys like you. It's only until November; then we will make the arrests and you will be back to your office job."

"November? Chief, with all due respect, I took this job knowing I would be home every night. You know why I'm here. Who's going to look after her?" I was shocked.

"Gavin, this isn't a request. I know you're worried about Payton. Evan will continue to trail Chad and I will check on her daily. I've already arranged for dispatch to drive her to doctor appointments whenever necessary."

I roughly ran my hand down the length of my face. How could this be happening? It had only been a week since I'd made a breakthrough with Payton. She trusted me enough to let herself want me, to let herself need me. Now I wasn't going to be there. I was going to leave her, just like everyone else did.

"What if I say no?" I asked Daniel without making eye contact.

"We don't have to worry about that, Sparks. Take the rest of the week off. Be here Sunday at 9 for your prep."

I walked out of his office with my thoughts in a fog. I knew I couldn't say no; it's my job and this was an important case. Too important to risk screwing it up.

Shit.

***

Payton was painting her nails at the kitchen table when I walked in. She was in a pair of yoga pants and one of my t-shirts.

"Hey, you're home early," she said. I nodded at her and forced a smile I knew didn't reach my eyes. I walked to the bathroom and locked the door before getting in the shower. I was rinsing the shampoo out of my hair when I heard the doorknob jiggle. I never locked the door, but I needed a little longer to get myself together.

She was sitting on the edge of my bed waiting for me when I walked in with a towel around my waist.

I knew I had tears in my eyes and I hated myself for letting her see them.

"Gavin, what's wrong? What happened?" she asked, coming to me.

I wrapped my arms around her and pulled her against me. My chest and back were still damp from the shower, but I couldn't *not* touch her, knowing that I only had three days left with her.

"I need to talk to you about something, Payton. I need you to stay calm and try to understand, okay?"

She started shaking her head and pushing against my chest. "No, not okay. You're leaving, Gavin. I can tell by the look on your face!"

She grabbed her keys off of the dresser and ran out of my room. I ran after her and pushed the front door shut from behind her. "Move!" she yelled.

"It's not what you think, Payton. I'm going undercover. I don't want to leave you; I have to. It's only temporary." She was quiet for a second. When I saw her hand fall from the doorknob, I felt an inkling of hope that she'd stay and let me explain.

"What kind of undercover?" she whispered.

"You know I can't tell you that. I don't want to put you in any danger. Some of the uni's are going to look after you while I'm under. They're going to take you to your appointments, too."

"I don't want them to look after me. And I can take myself to my own appointments, Gavin. Stop acting like I'm the one in danger; you're the one going undercover."

"I know you can handle it on your own, Payton, but I can't leave you not knowing that you're going to be okay until I get back."

She turned around to face me. She had tears in her own eyes now. "When will that be?" she asked, looking into my eyes.

"November," I sighed.

I could tell that she was thinking, calculating how long I would be gone. When she realized it was two months away, she gasped and more tears fell down her cheeks. I put my hands on her face and used my thumbs to wipe her tears away before pulling her into my kiss. She grabbed onto my shirt and clung to it. I picked her up and she wrapped her legs around me, knocking my towel loose in the process. I let it fall to the ground before walking her to the bedroom. I spent the rest of the night showing her how much I loved her, but only telling her how much I would miss her. I knew she wasn't ready to hear more than that, not yet.

***

The next three days went by even faster than I'd imagined. Payton agreed to stay at my place so Daniel would be able to check in on her occasionally. It took some convincing, but she also agreed to let one of the guys drive her to her appointments as long as they waited in the car. I'd seen Payton crying a couple of times since that first night, and it broke my heart. I was already counting down the days until I would be back with her.

We had gone to her house and gotten the rest of her clothes and most of the baby clothes we had bought together. She said that washing and folding all of the clothes would help keep her busy. I didn't have the heart to tell her that there couldn't have been more than two loads of laundry altogether.

We were on our way to Daniel's office in my truck when Payton caught me by surprise by grabbing my hand and squeezing it tight. I glanced at her, but she was looking out her window.

"Gavin, promise me something," she said without looking at me.

"What is it?"

"Promise you won't worry about me. I don't want you to get hurt because you're not focusing."

"I'm going to be fine, Payton. You promise not to worry about me, and I'll do the same."

"I can't make that promise," she said, shaking her head.

I brought our hands up to my lips and kissed her knuckles. "Neither can I," I told her as I put the truck in park. We walked up to Daniel's office without saying anything else.

"Hello, Gavin. It's nice to finally meet you, Payton. I promise to take care of the big guy for ya," Daniel told her as he slapped me on the back. She forced a smile and muttered a "thanks."

"Give us just a minute, Chief." Daniel nodded and walked out of his office, closing the door behind him.

As soon as the door clicked, Payton threw her arms around my neck and buried her face in my chest.

"I miss you already," I told her as I kissed her hair.

"I'm going to be here when you get back. I'm not going anywhere, Gavin." She had agreed to stay at my place, but I knew there was a chance of her second guessing the feelings we have for each other. I wouldn't be there to remind her that it's the real deal, and she would go running back to her house to be Miss Independent. I needed to hear her say those words. I took a moment to burn them into my memory. I knew I would need to refer back to them over the next two months.

After kissing Payton and wiping her tears, I watched her walk away, taking my heart with her.

I was sitting in the chair in front of Daniel's desk with my head in my hands when he came back in.

"Time will go by faster than you think, Gavin," he said as he leaned against his desk. I didn't even look up at him. I just acted like he'd said nothing at all.

"Shall we prep then?" he asked after clearing his throat. I nodded, reluctantly.

"You already know Dino is in deep. He's running with the guys that go to Rick Granger directly. We are hoping he will be able to befriend Rick and get the exact date of the upcoming shipment. You don't know Dino; if you see him and get introduced, you do not like him and do not act friendly towards him."

"Chief, you do realize I've done this before, right?" I cut him off.

He smirked and nodded. "I'll cut to the chase then, Sparks. You'll be the delivery boy for Granger. You'll transport drugs and weapons for him. Keep your head in the game and this will be over before you know it. You'll meet a group of the boys at a warehouse downtown at midnight. Good luck." He shook my hand before walking out, and I rolled my eyes at his casualness. Like everything would be fine and there was no chance of our cover being blown and the case being a bust. *Bullshit.*

Payton

One week without Gavin. One week of crying, wallowing, and worrying. One week of misery. Seven weeks to go.

I wadded my hair up and wrapped a ponytail around it. I didn't want to put makeup on, but I didn't want Dr. Grey asking questions about how I was feeling. So I did my best to look the same as I did at every other appointment.

I was waiting outside by my Jeep when a black truck pulled up to the curb. An officer got out of the driver's seat and came around to offer me his hand.

"Hello, Payton. I'm Cory. I'll be escorting you to your appointment today."

I shook his hand and muttered a "thank you" before climbing into his truck. Cory looked to be in his mid-thirties. His hair was a mixture of black and grey. I wasn't sure what it was about him, but I trusted him instantly.

"I'm glad we aren't taking a patrol car," I told him as he shut his own door.

"Gavin told me to bring an unmarked vehicle. He said you wouldn't want the unnecessary attention."

He was right. I looked out the window and tried not to think about where he was and what he was doing as we made the hour long drive to Dr. Grey's office.

Cory dropped me off at the entrance and went to park the truck. I was relieved that I didn't have to ask him to wait in the truck; he already knew that's what I wanted. Thanks to Gavin.

The nurse called me back within ten minutes. After checking my weight and blood pressure, she left me in an exam room to wait for the doctor. Thankfully, the wait wasn't very long.

"Hello, Payton. How are you feeling?" Dr. Grey asked as she shook my hand.

"I feel fine. A little tired, but I'm getting used to feeling that way," I said with a forced smile.

"Unfortunately, that is normal. I am a little concerned about your blood pressure, though.

It's a little too high for my liking. Have you been stressed lately?"

"Maybe a little," I answered her.

"Let's check the baby's heart rate. As long as she's doing okay, then we will just keep your regular appointment in two weeks."

I nodded and lay back on the table. Dr. Grey tugged my t-shirt up over my belly and I closed my eyes so I could focus on the sound that came from the monitor.

Too soon, she turned it off and wiped the gel off of me. "Everything sounds great, Payton. Get plenty of rest, and up your water intake for me, okay?"

I agreed, and she walked me up to the desk. After confirming my next appointment, I walked out to the parking lot to look for Cory. I spotted him in the truck after a moment. He was parked in the furthest row of spots. I inwardly groaned at having to walk that far. I hoped he would look up and see me so he would pull the truck around, but his eyes were glued to the cellphone in his hands.

"Hello, Haley," I heard from behind me. I shouldn't have, but out of habit, I turned to see who had called my name. My old name.

"You must be mistaken, I'm Payton. Remember?" I asked as Chad Granger and two other men started walking toward me.

"Oh, I remember all right. Haley Golds. Born and raised in Los Angeles. Daughter to one of our greatest customers: Rob Golds."

I swallowed the lump in my throat and tried to keep my voice as steady as possible. "I've never been to L.A., Chad. And I don't know anyone with the last name Golds. I was raised in Oklahoma. My father's name was Mike."

He laughed and kept walking toward me. Once he was within reaching distance he grabbed my arm, just above the elbow. "That's a nice little story, Hales," he bit out. "But I know the truth. I knew I recognized you from somewhere. Now, tell me, where is Sanford at these days?"

I tried to pull my arm out of his grasp and he squeezed it tighter. I let out a yelp of pain as he jerked me closer to him.

"Is there a problem here, fellas?"

I turned to see Cory walking towards us, rolling his sleeves up over his forearms.

"Payton, you know these guys?" he asked me. I could feel Chad squeeze my arm tighter, as if he were warning me to say what I needed to say to get rid of Cory. Still, I shook my head *no*.

"Well, then, I suggest y'all move along and we will call this all a misunderstanding," Cory said, staring at Chad.

"Big mistake, Beautiful," Chad whispered in my ear before releasing my arm and shoving me toward Cory.

Thankfully, Cory was quick on his feet and grabbed me before I fell on the concrete. "You okay?" he asked.

"Fine. Let's get out of here," I mumbled.

"I'm sorry I didn't see you walk out. I'm sorry I wasn't waiting for you by the door. I'm sorry I took so long."

"One apology is enough Cory. I'm fine and it's over. Let's forget about it," I told him as he pulled up to the curb outside of Gavin's apartment.

"Well, if that bruise is still on your arm when Gavin gets back, it will not be fine and it will be far from over." Cory closed his eyes and shook his head. I knew he felt terrible for letting the one guy I'm supposed to be protected from get to me on his watch.

"Gavin will never know, I promise. Thank you for keeping me company today. I'll see you in two weeks." I gave him a light hug before getting out of the truck and bolting to the apartment door.

I locked the door behind me and leaned against it. I tried to blink away the tears, but it was no use. The stress of the morning had caught up to me, and coming home to Gavin's empty apartment made things even worse. Not to mention the pregnancy hormones that had me crying at the drop of a hat these days.

My back was aching and I could feel a tightening sensation in my lower belly. I knew my blood pressure had to be even higher now than it was at Dr. Grey's office. After wiping my tears, I grabbed a bottle of water and went to run myself a warm bath.

The weird feeling in my stomach subsided as I relaxed, but the pain in my back stayed well into the night. I tossed and turned in Gavin's bed, unable to find a comfortable position. I finally dozed off after two in the morning.

***

"Haley!" My father called. "Can you come down here for a moment?"

"Coming, Daddy!" I answered as I put my diary under my pillow and jogged down the stairs. Daddy was waiting by the front door for me. "There's some people that want to meet you," he told me.

He put his hand on my shoulder as he opened the door and walked me out onto the porch. A man and a boy around my age were outside. "Rick, this is my daughter, Haley," my dad said to the man.

"Ah, it's nice to finally meet you, Haley. This is my son, Chad. Why don't the two of you go play while your daddy and I take care of some business, okay?" I nodded and the boy grabbed my hand and started pulling me back inside the house.

"Want to go in the backyard?" I asked. He shrugged his shoulders as if he didn't really want to go anywhere with me. I shrugged mine, too, and walked through the kitchen and out the back door. He didn't follow me. I had been outside alone for a good ten minutes before he finally came outside and sat next to me on the porch swing. "My dad says I have to be your boyfriend," Chad said.

I raised my eyebrow at him and laughed. "I already have a boyfriend. He's fourteen. You don't want to mess with him," I warned.

"I ain't afraid of no fourteen year old," Chad
said confidently. *"Don't worry about it, anyway.
You're not pretty enough to be my girl."* He hopped
off the swing and went back inside, letting the door
slam behind him.

What a jerk, I thought.

I was pretty. Sean told me all the time.

I woke up with my heart pounding. That's
why Chad thought I looked familiar the first
time he saw me at the steakhouse. How could I
have forgotten?

Gavin

"G! Get your ass in here!" I heard one of the boys who had been assigned to look after me yell. I got up off of the ratty old couch I'd slept on and walked into the kitchen. If you could even call it a kitchen. I'd spent the last four weeks staying in this rundown, piece of shit house. Half of the windows were busted out, there was no such thing as air conditioning, and I had to fight the mice for breakfast scraps.

"Well, look who finally decided to wake up," K said, mocking me as I stretched. We only called each other by the first letter of our names, which I liked. I didn't want to have to memorize the names of these low-lifes.

"What can I do for you, K?" I asked. He threw a black bag at my chest. I tried to catch it, but the damn thing was full of something and heavier than I'd anticipated. It fell to the ground after effectively knocking the breath out of me.

"Pick that up, for starters." K threw his head back and laughed like he was the funniest dude on the planet. I gritted my teeth and bent over to pick up the bag, reminding myself to play nice. For now.

"That load needs to be dropped off at Chad's place before dawn. Think you can handle that, Dipshit?"

"I would probably do a better job if you told me where Chad lived, K."

He stopped stuffing the other bag that was in front of him and stalked towards me. "You got an attitude this mornin', G?" he asked, pressing his chest against mine. He'd done this countless times. I couldn't decide if he was trying to scare me or trying to piss me off so he'd have a reason to shoot me. Unfortunately, he was getting closer to success with the latter.

"Back up, K. Give me the address and I'm out of here," I said, clenching my fists.

"And what if I don't back up? What're you gonna do?"

"I have a feeling you're going to find out pretty quick," I said, not backing down.

"Chad's house is over on Merchant Drive. Last house on the left. Don't fuck this up, G."

I stared at him for another second before tossing the black bag over my shoulder and walking out the door.

It was my fourth week being undercover. For some reason, they'd taken a liking to me. I was already getting to go to Chad's place. The next step up would be getting access to Rick's.

I drove toward Merchant Drive and had to force myself not to drive by my apartment complex. It was three in the morning, so I knew Payton would be there. If I drove by and saw her Jeep out front, I knew I wouldn't be able to keep driving. I would have to stop and go in to see her. Then, who knows how long it would take me to leave her again.

I also knew there was the possibility of them putting a tracking device in the bag or on my vehicle, and I wouldn't risk putting her in danger. No matter how much I missed her.

I pulled up to Chad Granger's house and was relieved to see the porch light on. At least someone was expecting me. As soon as the door to my truck slammed shut, the door to the house opened. Some buff guy was waiting for me. Well, more than a buff guy. I like to consider myself pretty buff, but this guy was three times my size. I knew he had to be a bodyguard of some sort.

"Who the hell are you?" he asked as I walked up the steps toward him.

"Name's G. Just trying to make a delivery."

"What's in the bag?" he asked, narrowing his eyes at me.

"Didn't open it, man. Just dropping it off to Chad."

"Smart man. I'll take you to him."

I nodded and followed close behind him as we walked through the mansion of a house.

"You'll have to be patient with Chad tonight. He's been doing some drinking."

"Sounds like my kinda guy," I lied. The bodyguard smirked as he opened a door and put his arm out, directing me inside.

After walking into the room I saw four guys huddled around a computer. Three were standing and one was in a chair directly in front of the screen. The one in the chair was Chad. I had never seen the rest of them. I could feel my anger rising just at the thought of Chad going near Payton.

"What did you bring us?" one of the guys asked as he started walking toward me.

"Not a clue. I didn't open it," I told him.

"What kind of man makes a delivery in the middle of the night and doesn't peek inside to see what he's delivering?" the same guy questioned.

"I guess the kind that doesn't give a shit as long as he gets paid."

He cocked a brow at me and I knew I was pissing him off. *The feeling is mutual,* I thought to myself.

"See? That's her!" Chad yelled, pointing at the computer screen.

The guy that had been staring me down rolled his eyes and groaned. "Enough about Haley Fuckin' Golds, Chad. She ain't ever gonna want your ass."

Chad stood up from the chair and started saying something to the guy in front of me, but I didn't catch it. I was too busy walking over to the computer to pay attention.

The obituary for Haley Golds was pulled up on the screen. Complete with a picture of her and her parents. I drew my brows together and tried to piece together the conversations going on around me. Before I could catch up, one of the other guys I didn't know opened a different page on the screen. Hundreds of pictures of Haley flooded the screen.

After looking over them as quickly as possible I noticed her growing belly throughout the pictures. These weren't of Haley Golds. They were of Payton. My Payton. Chad knew her, and he knew who she used to be.

"I would back up if I were you, man. Chad isn't interested in sharing this one," the guy who I'd handed the bag to said. I blinked a couple of times and tore my eyes from the screen.

"What makes her so special?" I asked through gritted teeth. Attempting to keep calm.

"You mean aside from the fact that her parents left her with more money than the president?" Chad slurred.

"Lots of girls have money. Why not find one without the baggage?" I asked patting my stomach so he would know I was referring to the baby. The beautiful baby that I'd already seen inside of her perfect mother. The baby that I'd felt move countless times. The baby that I loved with all of my heart without even meeting her.

"Oh, she won't live long enough to have the baby. Just long enough to give me the money," he laughed. The mother fucker actually laughed.

I saw red, and it was over before anything started.

Payton

"Cory, what are you doing here?" I asked after answering the knock at the door.

"You seemed upset after your appointment yesterday. I just wanted to come by and check on you. I brought Chinese," he said with a cheesy grin.

"Thanks. Come on in," I said with a forced smile.

He sat the carry out on the kitchen counter and washed his hands in the sink. He'd taken me to two doctor's appointments and had come to check on me at least once a week since Gavin had left. He was a good guy and I enjoyed the company, but when he left I felt even lonelier than usual.

"So, how are you holding up?" he asked as he dried his hands.

"I'm fine," I shrugged. He handed me a container of food and walked to the couch. I sat down beside him and took a bite.

"You want to tell me what happened at your appointment yesterday? Are you mad that I waited in the lobby for you? I know you don't want me there, but I can't take any chances of Chad Granger finding you while I'm not around," he said in a rush.

"I'm not mad. I'm glad you came inside, Cory."

"Then what's got you so down? More so than usual."

"Dr. Grey thinks I'll go into labor early. I've been having a lot of back pain over the past couple of weeks, and my blood pressure is a little high. If it's still high in two weeks, then I'll have to be induced."

"But Gavin won't be here in two weeks. He's still got four weeks to go, and that's if everything goes as planned." Cory looked at me and stopped talking once he saw the tears in my eyes.

"I know the baby isn't Gavin's, and he's not obligated to be there for the birth. But, the thought of doing it without him is terrifying."

Cory hugged me and got up to get me a tissue. "I'm going to talk to Daniel tomorrow and see if I can get any information on Gavin. Try not to worry. I'll call you tomorrow."

I nodded, and he took his container of Chinese with him as he left. I didn't blame him. I wouldn't want to have dinner with me right now either.

I pulled myself together and continued eating. When I was finished I took a warm bath. I'd been taking warm baths daily to help dull my back pain. I also bought a heating pad and slept with it on my back. The truth was, I wanted to have the baby. I wanted to not be pregnant anymore. But I wanted Gavin to be here for all of it. I needed him to be here for it.

I fell asleep on the couch watching TV. A loud banging sound woke me up. I glanced toward the window. It was light outside but I had no clue what time it was. I heard the banging sound again and realized it was at the door. Someone was knocking very loudly.

I looked through the peephole and saw Cory and Daniel on the other side of the door. I opened it instantly.

"What's wrong?" I asked nervously.

Cory grabbed my face and looked me over. "Are you okay?" they asked at the same time.

"I'm fine," I said, pushing Cory's hands away. "Why are the two of you here so early?"

"Early? Payton, it's one in the afternoon. We've been trying to call your cell."

My eyes widened at the realization that I'd slept for so long. I wasn't even sure where my phone was at the moment. I was ready to apologize for worrying them until I put everything together. I felt the color drain from my face.

"Why were you trying to call me?" I whispered. They both looked at me with sad looks on their faces.

"Payton, why don't you come with us? We will explain in the car," Daniel said.

I took a wobbly step toward them and Cory grabbed my arm, helping me walk to the black truck he usually picked me up in. He helped me into the passenger seat and walked around to the driver's side while Daniel got in the back.

I felt dizzy. I put my head in my hands and tried to breathe. Tried to calm my nerves. "Tell me," I begged.

"Gavin's been in an accident, Payton. We are taking you to him," Daniel told me as he put his hand on my shoulder.

"What kind of accident?" I asked with my hand over my mouth.

"He can explain more when you see him," Cory said.

I wiped the tears from my cheeks and twisted my hands in my lap. I was getting to see him. Four weeks earlier than we had planned. I wanted to be excited. I wanted to be happy to see him, but I could tell by the looks on the faces of Cory and Daniel that something was wrong.

We pulled up to the building that Daniel and Gavin's offices were in. I got out of the truck before Cory put it in park. I ran into the building and went straight to Gavin's office. He wasn't in there, but the light was on so I assumed he would be back soon.

Tears came to my eyes when I saw the ultrasound picture I had given him taped to the bottom of his computer. I rubbed my stomach as I let myself picture him being in the delivery room with me. Him holding her and calling her his own. A tear rolled off of my cheek and landed on a stack of papers on his desk. I tried to wipe it away quickly, but it made a dark spot on a tan folder. I picked it up to see if I had messed up something important.

My eyes widened when I read the name at the top of the file. I opened it and several pictures fell out onto his desk. They were of me growing up. My parents, Josh, Sean, they were all in them. This file was from my life in L.A. Haley Golds' life.

"I can explain," Gavin said as he came into his office with one arm in a sling and the other raised halfway in the air as if he were surrendering.

"You knew? You've known this whole time? You swore you weren't here to babysit me, Gavin!" I felt light-headed. I tried to reach for the chair in front of Gavin's computer, but I caught sight of the ultrasound picture again and stumbled. I heard my head hit the edge of his wooden desk before I felt the pain.

"Payton! Are you okay?" Gavin asked, rushing to my side. "You're bleeding," he said, getting on his knees to get a better look. He gently grabbed my chin and tried looking into my eyes, but I jerked away.

"Stop calling me Payton! My name is Haley! You know that!" I yelled.

"Baby, just let me explain. I can explain. Don't be upset, please. I've missed you so much. I've missed both of you," he said, resting his hand on my stomach.

"I'm not your baby and neither is she," I said quietly.

I got to my feet and walked out of his office. Leaving him on his knees with his head in his hand.

"Payton, there are still some things we have to go over. Please have a seat," Daniel said.

I sat down and looked at him expectantly. I heard two sets of footsteps enter his office behind me. I knew it was Cory and Gavin, but I kept my eyes trained on Daniel.

"Payton, you're being relocated. Temporarily, of course. Just until Gavin is finished with this case."

My mouth fell open and I felt like crying for the hundredth time in the last two hours.

"My fiancé is going with you, Payton. We are sending you both to Miami for the next four weeks. You will get to have fun and not have to worry about the shit going on here," Cory said, making me feel a little better.

"What happened? What does this have to do with me? Why am I being relocated and why is Gavin going back undercover if he's hurt?" I asked in a rush.

"I made a mistake," Gavin said quietly. "I let Chad know that I knew you. That you were important to me. He and his guys roughed me up a bit and warned me to stay away from you. My cover isn't blown; they think I'm here for questioning about the shooting."

"Shooting?" I asked without looking at him.

"They shot me after I hit Chad."

I jumped out of my seat and turned to look at him. "You got shot?" I asked. He shrugged like it wasn't a big deal. I took a deep breath and asked the other guys to leave us alone for a moment. Once they were out and the door was shut, I turned back to Gavin.

"Tell me the truth, Gavin. All of it."

"I was a detective in L.A. I worked several cases involving your father, Josh, and Sean. I've known who you were since your senior year in high school. I was there the night your parents were murdered. I helped you climb out of that tree and held your trembling body while we waited for the ambulance to arrive. You were in shock and started convulsing. You stopped breathing and I had to do CPR. I knew I wasn't doing the chest compressions hard enough, but I couldn't. I couldn't risk hurting your baby. You started breathing on your own just as the paramedics got there. The next day, my captain told me they were forcing you to change your identity and moving you to Alabama. A week after that, I put in for a transfer to come here. Not because I had to and not because I felt obligated to do anything."

"Why did you get shot?" I asked as I sat down in the chair again. I subtly took a deep breath and tried to relax. I could feel my stomach tightening again and I knew I was too stressed out.

"Chad and his friends were talking about him wanting you. I got pissed and threw a few punches. There were four of them and one of me. I got shot in the arm. It's not a big deal, Payton. I'm fine."

"I know you're fine; I can see that," I said, breathing heavily.

"Why are you so upset then?" he asked, walking toward me.

I shook my head and he stopped walking. Pain was radiating through my back.

"Payton, I know I should have told you I knew about your past. I just couldn't find the right time. I didn't want to scare you. Please don't be mad at me," he begged.

I squeezed my eyes shut and clenched my fists. "Gavin, I'm not mad. We can talk about it later. I need to go to the hospital," I said, breathing heavily. He finally understood and rushed to my side.

"Somebody call an ambulance!" he shouted. "Is it the baby? Are you in labor?" he asked me.

I shrugged and tried to breathe as normal as possible.

"A bus is on the way," Cory said as he jerked open the door. "What's going on?"

"I don't know. I think she's in labor," Gavin told him.

"Shit! I should have thought of that. The doctor told her yesterday she needed to keep her blood pressure down. They talked about inducing her early because it was too high," Cory told Gavin.

"You didn't think that was something I needed to know?" Gavin bit out.

"It's. Not. His. Fault," I gasped.

Gavin

"Sir, are you the father?" a nurse asked me. I hesitated and considered lying to her so she would let me see Payton. Cory put his hand on my shoulder and shook his head at me.

"No, I'm not the father," I muttered as I turned to go to the waiting room. The paramedics had told me they were going to call Dr. Grey and let her know that Payton was going to the hospital in Birmingham. They wouldn't let me ride with her, and now the nurse wouldn't let me in her room.

"Will someone just tell me what the fuck is going on?" I snapped.

I hadn't been asking anyone in particular, but Daniel answered me. "The nurse knows to fill us in as soon as she can, Gavin. Keep your head." I rested my good elbow on my knee and put my head in my hand.

An hour passed and I still hadn't heard anything from that nurse. Daniel went back to his office to figure something out for the Granger case. I told him there was no way I was going back undercover right now. Cory was still at the hospital, but he had gone to the cafeteria to get himself a coffee.

"Gavin?" I heard someone say my name and stood up quickly. I saw Dr. Grey standing at the nurse's station motioning me to come to her.

"Hello, Gavin. How are you holding up?" she asked.

"That doesn't matter. How is Payton?" I asked, irritated that she didn't start the conversation by telling me she was okay.

"She's fine, Gavin. She's resting."

"What's wrong with her? Why was she in so much pain? Is she in labor?"

Dr. Grey put her hands up to stop my line of questioning. "She was in premature labor. We've given her some medicine to stop the contractions and it is working well. She should be released by tomorrow morning, but she will be on bed rest once she gets home." I took a deep breath and willed myself to relax a little. She was okay and the baby was okay.

"Okay, I can take care of her," I said confidently.

"I will need to see her once a week until it's time to deliver the baby." I nodded, letting her know I could handle it. Without saying goodbye, she turned and walked back down the hallway. I went back to the waiting room to let Cory know Payton was okay. He was relieved and happy to go home to his fiancé. He took me to my apartment so I could change clothes and get my truck. I was back in that waiting room no more than an hour later.

I must have dozed off because I woke up when I felt someone tapping my shoulder. "Sir, are you Gavin Sparks?" the elderly nurse asked quietly. I blinked a couple of times, trying to remember where I was. When the realization hit me, I jumped out of my seat and said, "Yes ma'am," louder than I'd intended. I looked down at the startled nurse and, regaining my composure, said, "Yes, I'm Gavin Sparks." She nodded and then grinned at me. "Well, I appreciate your enthusiasm, Mr. Sparks. Please follow me."

I followed her down the bright hallway until she stopped in front of a door. "She's free to leave. She wanted to call a taxi, but I let her know you had been waiting all night."

"Thank you," I told her before opening the door to the hospital room.

Payton was sitting cross legged on the bed when I walked in. She was dressed in the same clothes she'd had on yesterday, but her hair was wet from her shower. She gave me a weak smile before trying to scoot herself off the bed. I took two quick strides to her and grabbed her hand to help her down.

"Thanks," she mumbled before walking into the hallway.

"I'm parked out this way," I said pointing toward the nearest exit. She nodded and followed me to my truck. She was silent the whole way to my apartment, and I could tell she was lost in her own head. After I parked the truck, she used her key to let herself in. By the time I had caught up with her, she was in my bedroom shoving her things into a bag.

"Oh, no you don't, Payton," I said as I snatched the bag away from her.

"Give it to me, Gavin. I'm going to my own house."

"Okay. Let me get my things and I'll go with you."

"I'm going alone," she said, sounding exasperated.

"Not a chance, Payton. I'm not going so I can take care of you, and I'm definitely not going to wait on you hand and foot while you're on bed rest. I'm going because I'm lonely and miserable without you." I didn't bring up the fact that Chad Granger still knew where she lived and still had his sights set on her. I was trying to cheer her up, not bring her down even more.

She dropped the t-shirt she had been holding and sat down on my bed. Her head was down, so I didn't realize she was crying until I heard her sniff a couple of times.

I sat down beside her and pulled her to me with my good arm. I kissed her hair as I waited for her to open up to me.

"I'm tired of being pregnant, Gavin. People aren't meant to do this alone. I'm supposed to have friends and a mom to help me through this," she said as she wiped her face with the back of her hand.

"I know you're tired, babe. You've had a long couple of days. Let's just stay here tonight and relax. We can go to your place tomorrow if that's what you want. Okay?"

"When are you leaving again?" she asked as she looked up at me with tears still in her eyes. I stared into her eyes while I considered my answer. I still hadn't heard anything from Daniel, so I wasn't sure if he had figured anything out. Regardless, I knew I wasn't going to go back under. Even if he needed me, she needed me more.

"I'm not going back undercover, Payton. I'm staying right here." When she wrapped her arms around me and hugged me tight, I knew I had made the right decision.

We spent the weekend at my place, only leaving the bedroom to go to the bathroom or to get food. I knew Payton was bored and tired of propping her feet up all day, but she hadn't complained since that first night.

"Do you want to stay at my place tonight?" she called from the couch. I was in the kitchen making lunch while she watched the *Lifetime* channel.

"Sure. We can leave after we take a nap."

"Can we stop by and eat with Gretta?"

"If you eat fast and promise to lay down the second we get to your house," I teased.

"Deal!" she yelled and I laughed.

We ate lunch on the couch in front of the TV. I waited for Payton to go lay down before I did the dishes and made sure the door was locked. Then I joined her. I tried not to let her see that I was still worried about Chad finding her; she didn't need the stress right now. Evan called to check in with me every evening. I just had to keep her safe until they were able to make the arrests, then we could both relax.

Payton woke up and rushed to the bathroom to shower. She was excited about getting out of the house for the first time in days, and I didn't blame her. I was ready to get some fresh air myself. Almost an hour later, Payton came into the kitchen. She was wearing a pair of skinny jeans and a dark green top that clung to her belly. She had taken the time to put on makeup and curl her hair, too. "Should I go change?" I asked her. "I didn't realize we were going all out for Gretta," I said with a wink.

"Yoga pants and hoodies are getting old. I just thought I would dress up a little now that I have somewhere to go," she said as her cheeks turned pink.

"You look great, Payton. We better go before I change my mind and keep you here to myself all night," I teased.

"Where is your sling?" she asked, raising her eyebrow.

"I feel fine, babe. I don't need it anymore."

She shrugged before planting a quick kiss on my lips and walking out the door. I took a second to appreciate her backside in the jeans she was wearing before following after her.

We were pulling into the parking lot of the café when Payton grabbed my hand. "Thank you. For everything," she said with a shy grin. I nodded and she gave my hand a squeeze before getting out of the truck and walking inside. I sat in the truck a moment longer trying to wipe the goofy grin off of my face. Payton was falling for me; I could see it in her eyes and hear it in her voice. I knew she wasn't ready to admit it to herself and definitely not to me, but just knowing it was happening made me the happiest man on the whole damn planet.

When I walked into the café, Gretta had her arms wrapped around Payton. I looked around for a place to sit. The place was usually empty, but today there were two booths occupied. I gave Gretta a quick hug and walked Payton to a table toward the back. "Gretta, I'll have water to drink and a cheeseburger with everything on it," I told her before walking to the other side of the small café to use the restroom. When I opened the door, there was another man standing there. I stepped back and to the side, holding the door open for him to leave, but he just stood there. I shrugged my shoulders and walked around him to the urinals. When I turned to wash my hands, I saw that he was still standing there, but he had turned around so he could see me. I narrowed my eyes at him and the hair started to stand up on the back of my neck.

"Do I know you?" I asked him as I tossed the paper towel I had used to dry my hands into the trash can.

"Not yet," he said in a raspy voice that made me think he smoked at least a pack a day. I took a second to take in his appearance, to see if anything about him seemed familiar. He was older than me by at least ten years. He was tall and thin—I had no doubt that I could take him — but I didn't want to cause a scene in front of Payton or make a mess inside of Gretta's café.

The man smirked at the confused look on my face and the uneasy feeling I had got worse. I brushed passed him and walked out the door. I shook my head, trying to forget the weird encounter I had just had before I got back to Payton.

When I looked up and saw that nobody was sitting at our table and that the other two tables were empty, fear shot through me. I walked to the back as quickly as possible. When I burst through the kitchen doors, I startled Gretta and made her drop a plate she had been drying. "Gavin, what's the matter? Your food will be right out; I know you need to get our girl home."

I felt like someone had punched me in the gut. I bent over and put my hands on my knees as I tried to catch my breath. The arm I was shot in throbbed from the extra weight I was putting on it, but I didn't care. "Where is she, Gretta? Did she tell you she was leaving?" I asked quietly, knowing she had no idea what I was talking about.

When I looked up again she was already walking by me to exit the kitchen. I followed her to the table Payton was sitting at and watched as she picked up a napkin studying it carefully. It was then that I saw the writing.

Gretta had a look of pure confusion on her face when she asked, "Who is Haley?"

My eyes grew wide and I grabbed the napkin out of her hand.

Gavin,

Thank you for all you have done. I can take it from here. I don't need your help anymore.

-Haley

I crumbled the napkin in my hand and shoved it in my pocket. When I looked at Gretta, she had tears in her eyes. "I'll find her," I whispered before walking out of the café.

I did my best to keep it together in front of Gretta. I wanted her to think that Payton had left me by choice, but I knew better. She had been taken, and I had a pretty good idea of who had her. It had to have been Chad and the boys. Why else would she have signed the note as "Haley?"

Evan picked up on the first ring.

"Gavin, I was just about to call you. I think the boys have something up their sleeve. I followed them out of Birmingham. They brought three trucks to Payton's house first. They all split up almost an hour ago. I'm on foot outside Payton's house, trying to see what their intentions are."

"They took her, Evan. We were at the café. I went to the bathroom. When I came out, she was gone," I said in a rush. "Where is Chad? I know they are taking her to him."

"Shit, Gavin. We'll find her. Chad was in one of the other trucks. A maroon one. I didn't tail him because I assumed y'all would be coming straight to her house. I thought this was the best place for me to be. Fuck, I'm sorry man. I'm almost back to my truck. Meet me at the steakhouse." I could tell Evan was running because he was breathing heavily into the phone. I pulled into the steakhouse parking lot and slammed my truck into park. I rested my head on the steering wheel as I waited for Evan to show up.

Payton

I blinked back tears as I sat in the backseat of Chad Granger's truck. I refused to let myself cry in front of him.

"You worried about your boyfriend, darlin'?" he asked, looking at me in the rearview mirror. When I didn't answer, he grinned. "Don't you worry your pretty little head; a deal is a deal. You came without a fight, so your man will leave without a scratch on him."

I forced myself to look out the window and away from his shit-eating grin. I hoped Gavin had caught on to the note I'd left him. Chad is the only other person that knows who I really am. I hope Gavin realizes from that that Chad's the one doing this.

My hands flew to my stomach and I sucked in a deep breath as pain radiated all around my abdomen. I breathed through the pain and my body started relaxing before Chad noticed I was uncomfortable. I kept my face as calm as possible. I knew if he saw that I was scared or hurt, he would use it to his advantage. I just had to be smart and stall until Gavin could catch up to us. *Please hurry, Gavin.*

"So, Haley, where is the money?" Chad asked in a sweet voice that made me feel sick.

"I don't have any money, Chad," I lied. Chad didn't hesitate before jerking the truck over and slamming it into park. He got out and opened the door to the back seat. I did my best to scoot away from him. My back was against the opposite door and my feet were in the seat. I had my knees pulled as close to my body as they would go.

Chad looked at me for a moment before a slow smile spread across his face. "You're scared, aren't ya?" I didn't move a muscle; I just stared right back at him. "You're lying to me, Haley. I know you've got your daddy's money. Where is it?" I narrowed my eyes at him before looking away. When he realized I still wasn't going to tell him, I heard him mutter, *"Bitch"* before grabbing both of my ankles and pulling me toward him. My head bounced off the door I had been leaning on. I kicked my feet as hard as I could, trying to get away from him. Once he was close enough, he grabbed my arms and hauled me out of the vehicle. My head slammed against the driver's side window as he pushed me into the side of the truck. I was pretty certain my head was bleeding and I didn't know how the window didn't break. I took in a deep breath and refused to let the tears, which were so desperately close to rolling down my cheeks, fall.

"I won't ask you again, Haley. Tell me," he spat. Another sharp pain shot through my stomach. This time it was impossible to hold back my tears. I squeezed my eyes shut tight and tried to breathe through the pain, but it wasn't letting up. Just when I thought it was over, another wave of pain came. I let out a high pitched squeal and doubled over in pain. I didn't know what had happened when I felt the pain on the right side of my face, but when Chad grabbed me by the hair and his face came into focus I knew he had hit me. I could see the anger in his face, and I knew I didn't have a choice. I couldn't wait any longer. I gave him the address to the bank that my money had been transferred to. After shoving me into the backseat and slamming the door, we were speeding down the highway again.

I used my hands to gently massage my stomach while I focused on my breathing. I tried my hardest to relax, but the pain kept coming, stronger and stronger.

By the time we turned onto the street the bank was on, I was light-headed and covered in sweat. I could hear Chad talking to someone, and I assumed he was on the phone because he didn't get mad when I didn't reply.

Even with my eyes closed, I could tell he had parked the truck by the way my body jerked forward and then back. I groaned out in pain at the unexpected movement.

"What the hell? How did he know we were coming here? Did you tip him off? You did, didn't you? You stupid bitch!" I could hear Chad yelling at me, but I had no clue what he was talking about and I couldn't focus long enough to find out. I heard his truck door slam right before everything went black. Right before I stopped feeling all of the pain. Right before I stopped feeling *everything*.

Gavin

"I know where they're going. Get in," I told Evan through the window of my truck. He nodded and grabbed his pistol out of his glove box before sprinting around to the passenger side of my truck. I didn't wait for him to get settled before peeling out of the parking lot and hauling ass to the bank that was a good twenty miles away. "Don't tell him, Payton. Don't you dare tell him!" I shouted, even though I knew she couldn't hear me.

"Dude, fill me in," Evan said quietly.

"Chad wants the money she got after her parents died. That's all he wants from her. Once he has what he wants, there will be no reason to keep Payton around. But he won't let her go, because she would be able to turn him in. He'll kill her when he's finished with her, Evan."

Evan swallowed hard and nodded. I pressed my foot harder onto the gas pedal and prayed like hell we would make it in time.

"I'm going to call Daniel and have him send backup. We're going to have to arrest Chad, and Dino needs a heads up so his cover isn't blown," Evan said as he pulled out his cellphone and started dialing.

"Have them send an ambulance. Tell them it's for a pregnant woman," I said with a shaky voice.

I pulled into the bank parking lot and nervously scanned all the other vehicles, looking for the maroon truck Evan had seen Chad driving.

"Evan, go inside and check with a teller. Make sure they haven't already been in there." He jumped out of the truck and ran inside without hesitating. I grabbed my gun and the extra pair of handcuffs out of my glove box. I got out of my truck and was tucking my pistol into the waist band of my jeans when I saw the maroon truck pull into the parking lot.

As I walked toward his driver's side door, I knew the exact moment Chad saw me. His mouth started moving quickly and he leaned over to get something out of his glove box. I had no doubt that it was a gun, but I still didn't grab for my own. There was no way I was going to let this fight end that quickly.

I squinted my eyes, trying to see through the back window. I needed to see Payton. I needed to know she was okay. As I got closer, I could see the reddish color of her hair splayed across the window as she leaned her head against it. I yelled her name at the top of my lungs, but she didn't move. She didn't even attempt to move. My whole body was vibrating with anger and fear at the thought of him hurting her.

The sound of Chad's truck door slamming brought my attention back to him. He was stalking toward me with his gun pointed right at my chest. Instead of stopping like I probably should have, I broke out into a sprint and headed straight for him.

I heard the gun go off at the same time as my body collided with his. We both fell to the ground and his gun slid across the concrete. I grabbed him by the shirt and pulled him about six inches off of the ground before slamming his head against the pavement again. I saw the dazed look in his eyes and knew I needed to stop. I knew that, but I didn't do it. I reared back and punched him in the jaw harder than I'd ever hit anything in my life. I could tell by the sounds that I had broken it. My hand was most likely broken as well.

"Sparks! We got company, man!" I heard Evan yell from across the lot. When I looked around I saw two other trucks parking beside Chad's truck. Within about thirty seconds five men were walking toward me with guns in their hands. The Granger Boys.

"Police! Put the guns down!" Evan yelled, but they kept walking without acknowledging him.

"I'll shoot! Put the weapons down!" he yelled again. Still, they kept walking.

I glanced down at Chad and realized his eyes were closed. After looking closer I saw that he was still breathing and realized he'd passed out. I unclenched my fist that was still holding his blood soaked shirt and started to slowly stand up. I had barely gotten to my feet when three patrol cars turned into the parking lot with their lights on and sirens blaring. I wasn't able to take a step before I heard the gun shot and felt the heat in my left side. I fell to my knees. Another shot went off and then the same heat was in my right shoulder, too. My vision started blurring and I couldn't hear anything. The next thing I knew, paramedics were lifting me onto a stretcher. "She's in the truck," I groaned. "Get Payton first." I didn't hear their response before I passed out from the pain.

Payton

"Payton? Dr. Grey is on her way. You don't need to worry about anything," a woman with long red hair told me. I blinked several times before realizing that the woman was wearing scrubs. She was a nurse and I was in the hospital. My head was killing me, but the pain I'd been feeling in my stomach had gone down to a dull throb. I looked at the IV in my left wrist and took a second to thank God for pain medication.

"How long have I been here?" I asked the nurse.

"You were brought in by ambulance an hour ago. Do you not remember anything?" she asked with her eyebrows raised.

I squinted my eyes in concentration. "I remember being at the bank with Chad. Did he call the ambulance?" I knew there was no way

Chad would have called them for me, but who else would have known where I was?

"I'm not sure who called them, Payton. I just know you got here just in time. We were able to start you on some mild pain medication and get your epidural started. Dr. Grey should be here any minute and we will get started." She was smiling at me as she patted my stomach. I started putting everything together and felt all the color drain from my face. "I'm having a baby? Tonight? Like, right now?" I said in a panicked voice.

"Yes, Payton, the baby is coming tonight. You're a little shy of eight months so there aren't as many risks as there are for babies that are born before seven months. However, we do have a helicopter on standby in case your baby needs to go to the children's hospital."

I felt my heart rate quicken and I started sweating. She must have been able to see how terrified I was because she went on trying to calm me down by telling me how great of a doctor Dr. Grey was. I stopped listening at some point and just started crying. The nurse finally gave up and left me alone to freak out in peace.

About twenty minutes later there was a knock on the door and Dr. Grey walked in. The red-headed nurse followed her along with another woman I hadn't seen before.

"Payton, how are you feeling?" Dr. Grey asked as she gave me a one armed hug.

"Scared," I mumbled.

"I understand, dear. We are going to take great care of you and your little girl, okay?"

I nodded and wiped the tears from my cheeks.

"Payton, I know we haven't had a chance to choose a pediatrician for your baby yet, but this is Dr. Brooke Duncan. I've asked her to be here with us tonight and to care for the baby until she is released from the hospital. Are you okay with that?"

I nodded again.

"Alright, then, let's get started. The nurse said you've been having steady contractions since the paramedics reached you. Are you feeling any of them now?" Dr. Grey asked as she put on a pair of latex gloves.

"I feel a little pressure, but no pain," I answered.

"That's good, Payton," she said with a smile. "Rebecca is going to pull your knees up for me so I can check you. If you are dilated enough, we will start pushing, okay?" I nodded as the nurse with red hair grabbed my feet and pushed them toward my head, causing my knees to bend.

A tear rolled down my cheek as I caught myself wishing my mother were here. I couldn't do this alone; *nobody* should have to do this alone. I told Gavin I couldn't do it; I told him. A sob broke out of me as I realized how much I needed Gavin to be here. "Where's Gavin?" I asked in a panic as I tried to sit up.

"Woah, Payton, just relax. Does Gavin know you're in the hospital?" Dr. Grey asked me.

"I don't know. I haven't seen him since we were at the café; that's where they took me. We were in the bank parking lot and I think Gavin was there. I think I heard him calling my name, but I couldn't see him. I never saw him," my voice broke.

"You were at the bank? The same bank where the shooting was at?" Dr. Duncan asked as she stepped closer to my side of the bed.

"What shooting?" Dr. Grey and I asked at the same time.

"Rebecca, call down to the E.R. and see if anyone was admitted with gunshot wounds. Payton, what is Gavin's last name?" she asked, ignoring our question.

"Sparks," I said as Rebecca hurried out of the room.

I leaned my head back and squeezed my eyes shut as the pressure in my lower belly intensified. "Ouchhhh," I groaned.

"Payton, you really need to push. I know you're scared, but you can do this," Dr. Grey said.

I opened my eyes and nodded as more tears rolled down my cheeks. "Push on three, okay?"

"Okay," I whispered as Dr. Duncan grabbed my hand.

"One. Two. Three!"

I pushed as hard as I could, and Dr. Grey encouraged me to breathe and do it again. She started counting, and before I had a chance to relax at all, I was pushing again.

"You're doing great, Payton. One more time and you will get to meet your baby girl. One. Two. Three!"

I pushed again and when I felt the pressure disappear I fell back onto my pillow. I hadn't seen Rebecca come back into the room, but there she was, wiping my face with a cool rag.

Moments later, I heard the sweetest little cry I've ever heard in my life. I propped myself up on my elbows and tried to get a better look, but Dr. Duncan was hovered over my bed with a thermometer and stethoscope and I was unable to see anything but her feet. Her perfectly tiny feet.

"Her lungs are weak, but she's doing a great job of breathing on her own right now. She will need to be monitored twenty-four hours a day for the next week, but if she keeps this up she shouldn't have any problems," Dr. Duncan said with a smile on her face.

"Payton, would you like to hold your daughter, now?" Dr. Grey asked me. I nodded, and she immediately handed me a small bundle of white blankets. I wouldn't have known my daughter was in there if I hadn't seen her dark brown hair sticking out of the top.

I pulled the blankets away so I could see all of her. She squirmed in my arms as the cool air hit her, and I put my hand over her chest to feel her heartbeat. She wrapped her tiny hand around my thumb, effectively melting my heart. After everyone had left the room, I laid my baby girl on my chest. Tears rolled down my cheeks as I felt her little puffs of breath against my neck. She was just born, but she was already so strong. More tears fell as I thought about Gavin and how proud of her he would be. He had never asked, but I knew how bad he wanted to be here for this. I knew how bad he wanted to claim this baby girl as his own. I cried all of the tears I had left as I held the most amazing thing I'd ever done in my arms.

Gavin

"Fuck," I groaned. "What happened?" I asked without opening my eyes.

"Well, Boss, ya got yourself shot. Again. Twice," Evan said. I blinked a couple times until my vision cleared. He opened his mouth like he was going to explain everything to me, but I shook my head at him because I remembered enough.

"Well, Payton-" Evan started. "Shit! What are you doing?" he shouted as I jolted upright and swung my legs over the side of the bed.

"Where is she?" I asked right before I pulled the IV out of my arm. "She's upstairs on the birthing floor, dude. Don't you think you should wait and see a doctor?" he asked.

"Did you bring me any clothes?" I asked, ignoring his question. He tossed a black Nike bag to me and I caught it with the arm that wasn't in a sling. After unzipping it, I saw a pair of sweats and a clean shirt. "She's in room 431, Gav. Go get her," he walked out, smiling and shaking his head.

I did my best to get dressed as quickly as possible. I was still in a lot of pain, but not enough to keep me in this bed, away from Payton. When I finally made it to the fourth floor, I had beads of sweat running down my back. I knew part of that was because of the severe pain I was enduring with every step I took and part of it was because I was anxious to see Payton, to make sure she was okay.

When I came to room 431, the door was cracked. I didn't bother knocking before I walked in. Payton was asleep on her back with one arm over her eyes blocking the light. She had a light pink blanket clenched in her other hand. After seeing the blanket, I noticed that her used to be swollen stomach was now flat. Almost as flat as it was before she had ever gotten pregnant. She'd had the baby, but where was she? I got a sick feeling in my stomach as I walked up to the side of the bed.

Forgetting about the searing pain in my side, I leaned over and kissed Payton's cheek. She moved her arm from her eyes and blinked up at me. "Gavin?" she whispered. "What are you doing here? You should be—" I cut her off by pressing my lips to hers.

"I'm so glad you're okay, Payton. I'm so sorry I wasn't here," I told her in between kisses. "I'm so sorry. So sorry, Payton."

"Gavin," she tried to say something but I couldn't stop kissing her. "I'm sorry," I whispered again as I blinked back the tears that were threatening to fall onto my cheeks.

"Gavin," she started again, but I kept kissing her and she kept returning my kisses.

Eventually, she put her hand between us and pushed against my chest. I stepped back, letting her sit up, before I leaned back in to kiss her forehead. "I'm so sorry you had to do this alone," I told her. My voice broke and she looked up at me confused.

"Gavin, I'm fine. She's fine. Everything is perfect," she said with tears in her eyes and a smile on her face. I took a step back as I replayed what she had just said in my head.

"She's fine?" I asked.

Payton nodded enthusiastically and giggled at the confused look on my face. She stood up and wrapped her arms around me loosely. "Would you like to meet her?" she asked. All I could manage was a nod. She walked me over to the bed and helped me sit down before leaving the room. I slid my sling off and laid it on the bed beside me. I might regret it later, but at the moment, I felt no pain.

My mind was still reeling when she walked back in carrying a tiny bundle of pink. I stopped breathing when she placed her in my arms. I looked up at Payton and saw the tears running down her cheeks; I knew she could see my own tears pooling in my eyes, but I didn't try to hide them.

"She's perfect," I whispered as I stared down at her. I never knew I was capable of loving someone so much until this moment. I loved this little girl and her mother with every part of my soul. I knew that from that moment on my world would forever revolve around them.

"What's her name?" I asked, without looking away from her. "Look at the bracelet on her ankle," Payton said quietly. I looked up at her to make sure it was okay to take the blanket off of her feet. She nodded and looked away. I could tell she was nervous, but I didn't know why. I was sure I would love whatever name she chose.

I gently uncovered her feet and smiled at the fluffy pink socks she was wearing. I held her left leg still and turned the bracelet so I could read her name.

Haley Belle Sparks

Tears fell freely down my cheeks as I said her name out loud.

"I think we should call her Belle, but I wanted to make her a part of me and a part of you. I hope that's okay," Payton said from across the room.

"I love you," I answered without hesitation. "I love you so damn much, Payton. And I love her. I always will."

Payton walked over and sat next to us on the bed. She used the back of her hand to wipe away my tears before saying, "I love you, too, Gavin," and pressing her lips to mine.

Payton

That night, after Gavin's doctor scolded him for leaving his room, the nurses set up another bed so he could stay in the room with us. I slept next to him in that tiny hospital bed, our daughter in a smaller bed of her own beside us.

We spent the next ten days in that room together. Belle's lungs were getting stronger every day and Gavin's wounds were healing. We were packing our things and getting ready to put Belle in her infant carrier when there was a knock on the door.

"Hey, man. Lookin' good," Evan said as he greeted Gavin with a pat on the back. Daniel walked in after him. After handing Belle over to Evan, I went to sit on the bed next to Gavin.

"What brings y'all out?" Gavin asked them.

"Well, Evan has baby fever apparently. He hasn't stopped talking about that little girl of yours for the last week," Daniel said with a grin. "I'm here to share some news with the two of you."

"What kind of news?" Gavin asked with raised eyebrows.

"Oh, nothing big, just that Rick and the boys are all behind bars," Evan cut in.

My jaw dropped and I stood up to hug Daniel. I was making my way over to Evan when he started backing away from me. I put my hands on my hips and cocked my head to the side.

"She's almost asleep," he whispered. We all laughed and I rolled my eyes at him.

"So what happened? How'd you get Rick?" Gavin asked, clearly happy with the good news.

"After he found out Chad got sentenced for twenty-five years to life, he got a little antsy, I guess. He moved the shipment up. Thankfully, Dino was one of his main guys. He was able to give us a heads up and we were waiting for them," Daniel explained enthusiastically.

"I know Rick will never get out, but what about the other boys?" Gavin asked as he wrapped his arms around me.

"They haven't been sentenced yet, man. But they're all being transferred to Cali. Apparently, they had warrants there, too. Sam was happy to take them off our hands," Evan told us.

"You hear that, babe? We get to go home, and we are going to stay there as long as you want," Gavin whispered to me. We breathed a sigh of relief together.

"Take us home," I told him.

Four years later

Gavin

I pulled into the driveway of our two story house. Belle's hot pink, battery operated Jeep was parked beside her mom's new red Jeep. I smiled as I remembered our argument about getting something that wasn't black. Payton had finally given in to Belle and me and gotten something red.

The door to our house opened before I could put my truck in park. "Daddy!" Belle squealed as she ran toward me. I smiled down at her before picking her up and placing her on my shoulders.

"How was your day, baby girl?"

"It was fun! Mommy helped me make a surprise for you. Hurry! Let's get inside!" she said clapping her hands.

I couldn't help but chuckle at her enthusiasm as we walked inside. I sat her down and watched her run through the house as I sat my keys and badge down on the small table that Payton had put in our entry way.

When I rounded the corner into the kitchen, Payton's back was to me as she did something on the stove. I walked up behind her and wrapped my arms around her waist before kissing her neck.

"What smells so good?" I asked her.

She giggled before saying, "That could be the chicken I have in the oven or the mud pie your daughter is making for your birthday dinner tonight."

"Ah, so that's my surprise, huh? That little girl makes the best mud pies," I laughed. "When will everyone be here?"

"Evan called. He's running late. Something about projectile vomiting and poopy diapers," she said with a smirk. "Daniel and Lacey are on their way and so is Gretta. Why don't you go change while you have time?"

I turned her around so she was facing me. I kissed her until I was certain she had forgotten about the food on the stove. "I would rather do something else, while I still have time," I said suggestively.

"We don't have that kind of time, Gavin. Go get dressed," she said, smacking my chest.

Payton

"I would say that birthday dinner was a success. What do you think, baby girl?" Gavin asked Belle.

"Best birthday dinner ever, Daddy," she said through a yawn.

Gavin smiled at me before carrying Belle to her bedroom. I finished putting the dirty dishes into the dishwasher as quickly as I could. I knew I didn't have much time before Gavin was finished telling Belle a story and putting her to sleep.

I walked down the hall to mine and Gavin's bedroom. I was extra quiet as I passed Belle's door so Gavin wouldn't know I was going to bed so soon.

I opened the drawer to my nightstand beside the bed and moved some things around until I found what I was looking for: the ultrasound picture Dr. Grey had given me at my appointment yesterday.

I had been nervous when I first found out I was pregnant. Gavin and I hadn't been trying to have a baby, but we weren't exactly preventing it, either.

I wanted to surprise Gavin tonight for his birthday, so I went ahead and had my first appointment without him. Dr. Grey was happy to help me with the surprise and offered to give me an ultrasound photo even though we normally wouldn't do an ultrasound for a few more weeks.

I heard Belle's door click shut and I jumped in the bed, getting under the covers as quickly as possible. I slipped the picture onto Gavin's pillow and did my best at pretending to sleep.

He opened the door and quietly walked to his side of the bed. As I heard him getting undressed, my heart rate sped up like it always did. When I felt him lifting the covers to crawl into bed, I couldn't hold back my smile anymore. It was dark and he couldn't see my face, thankfully.

I heard the crumble of the picture as he laid back onto his pillow. "What the?" I put my hand over my mouth to hold back my giggle. He turned on the lamp on his side of the bed, but I kept my eyes closed and my back turned.

"Payton? Are you? Is this real?" he asked quietly. I still didn't turn over.

"Babe, I know you're awake. Your giggling is shaking the bed," he said as he tugged on my shoulder, forcing me to roll over.

I gave him a full-on happy smile and tears formed in his eyes. "This is our baby?" he whispered.

"Coming this September," I said with an enthusiastic nod.

He sat the picture down on his nightstand and scooped me into his lap. "We're going to have a baby. Belle is going to have a little brother or a little sister," he said, excited.

"Happy birthday, baby," I said before pressing my lips to his.

"I love you," he muttered between kisses.

29346882R00138

Made in the USA
Columbia, SC
22 October 2018